The Frog Theory

Fiona Mordaunt

Published by Go-Away books 2019

Copyright © 2019

Second edition

The author asserts the moral right under the Copyright, Designs and Patents Act 1988 to be identified as the author of this work.

All rights reserved. No part of this publication may be reproduced, stored in a retrieval system or transmitted, in any form or by any means without the prior consent of the author, nor be otherwise circulated in any form of binding or cover other than that with which it is published and without a similar condition being imposed on the subsequent purchaser.

ISBN: 978-1-9996520-0-5 paperback
978-1-9996520-1-2 eBook

Printed and bound in Great Britain by
Clays Ltd, Elcograf S.p.A.

Dedicated to Diana Mather
For being generous, kind,
funny and loving.
thank you
My angel in the mist (or fog)

Contents

Before they all met   7
  IV Introductions   7
  I Kim   7
  II Clea   9
  III The principal   12
  IV Flow   14
The window incident   17
  Repercussions   19
  Probation   20
  Catching the train   22
  Gossiping girls   22
The fight   25
  Job interview   28
  The principal   30
  Chuck me a rope   30
  New Forest   31
  Later, in Ryan's tent   33
The party   34
  Inside Clea's house   41
  Flow's dilemma   43
The frog theory   45
Mr Whippy   56
  The solicitor   57
  Smash the mask   61
Smart shoes   64
  Must try harder   66
  The Ritz   67

Message in a bottle	72
Bad vibrations	73
Maybe baby	76
Worried sick	81
Leigh's pickle	84
Wake-up call	87
Going places	90
Testing natural chemistry	97
Why don't you join us for dinner?	102
Food fight goes viral	115
Gold	119
One-to-one	128
Secret's out	131
Flow	132
Coming clean	136
Resurrected	137
The kiss	142
Shhh. Listen to the rain	149
No more nightmares	151
Charlie	152
Epilogue	155

Before they all met

It was as if they had been carefully placed on invisible circuits, predestined to meet, in order to help each other.

IV Introductions

I

Kim

As Kim walked to Bishops Park from the council estate he lived on in Fulham, he stopped to light a cigarette, turning his back to the wind to shelter the flame that leapt and wriggled from his lighter. When darkness fell, the park was their illicit night-spot – all the kids from the surrounding council estates knew about it.

Kim slid through the gap in the fence, which was their entrance, and made his way to the playground area, where his friends tended to congregate. He wondered what his best mate, Flow, had done to upset his girlfriend this time, you could tell by her body language she was having a go.

'Ryan!' he shouted as he swung open the gate to the playground, deciding to give the arguing couple a wide berth. 'You buying?'

'Give me an eighth,' said Ryan, gratefully handing Kim some cash in exchange for the small package.

'Same,' said Pat, the scrawny guy standing next to him.

Kim looked around to see who else might be buying tonight.

The Frog Theory

The girls from his own estate might take a bit but they were whispering secretively, sitting on the wall by the paddling-pool – best left well alone for the moment.

Since it looked like Flow's girlfriend had stopped yelling, he opted to go in their direction next, greeting Flow with a manly slap on the back.

'He only went and smashed my watch,' Jackie complained, laying the heart of their argument bare.

'It said on the front it was shatterproof,' said Flow, defensively.

'And you put it to the test,' finished Kim.

If ever they went past a wet paint sign, Flow would stick his hand in the flagged area, and if there was a label saying 'fireproof' on anything, he'd put a flame to it and check. Kim had learnt Flow's peculiar logic over the years; it didn't matter whether material possessions were his or not – these impulsive acts were the norm. If Jackie hadn't worked that out during the time they'd been dating and was stupid enough to let him have her watch, well?

'He says "let me see your new watch", takes it off my wrist, looks at it and smashes it against the blimmin' wall,' lobbied Jackie.

'Which proves my point that it wasn't actually shatterproof, was it? And if I had *realised* it was going to smash, I wouldn't have done it, would I?'

'Sounds like misinformation on the part of the manufacturers to me,' said Kim, pledging allegiance to Flow. Jackie drew her mouth tight like a coin purse poised to spill.

'Looks like you're wanted, Jacks,' said Flow, nodding towards their friend Paula, who was waving wildly from her seat on the wall, face scrunched with determination. She was not what they would describe as attractive; hard as nails, too, perhaps to compensate.

Jackie dropped the argument in favour of gossip and spun away from them with a haughty flick of her hair.

'Skedaddle?' said Kim, once she was out of earshot. It was

the opportunity they needed to ditch her for the evening but Flow hesitated, undecided, lit a cigarette and stayed put.

That was the thing – Jackie had a hold over Flow. It was Friday night and the old Flow would have gone to the pub, played some pool, nicked a car. *Had a laugh.*

Kim just didn't get it.

II

Clea

Clea's stepfather, Hugo, had an unsettling habit of bursting into her room when her door was closed, as if he were trying to catch her naked and often, just as she was about to leave for school, he would find a reason to shout at her, making her late. This was one of those mornings.

'I want a word with you,' he said darkly, looming above her while she frantically crammed various bits of sports gear into her PE bag. He was brandishing a mug as if he had discovered stolen goods. 'It was in your bedroom,' he announced accusingly.

'Sorry, I'll put it in the dishwasher.'

Clea tried to take it from him but he held it out of her reach.

'That you choose to live like a slob is your own affair. That you choose to let it affect your mother and me is not. Why should we have to put up with your slovenliness?'

'You shouldn't,' she said meekly, eager to avoid a row and get to school on time.

'Your room is like a stinking boudoir, it makes the rest of the house smell,' he continued.

'I'll clean it when I get back,' she pleaded.

'Make sure that you do!' he snapped, finally relinquishing the mug.

She flung her bag to the floor and hurried down the long hall to the kitchen, loading the offensive item into the dishwasher as quickly as possible before turning to find him just behind her.

The Frog Theory

She took a sharp intake of breath. Whack! He had slapped her face.

'That's to ensure you don't forget,' he told her with a sneer.

She pushed past him, tears stinging her eyes, grabbed her things and made her escape. She slammed the front door as hard as she could and gave his stupid Porsche a hard kick as she passed it, too.

'I can't believe you're late again, Mr Berry's after your blood,' whispered Sarah.

'So, what's new?' Clea took her place at the desk beside her.

'I just thought after all the telling off you've had lately…It's not like you live that far away. Are you *trying* to get expelled?'

Clea unpacked her bag, deftly slapping an exercise book and pencil case onto the desk.

'You know, for a best friend you can really rub things in,' she said through clenched teeth.

'Hugo up to his normal tricks, then? What did he do this time?' Sarah asked eagerly.

Clea didn't answer. Sometimes she thought Sarah actually enjoyed hearing the grief Hugo put her through. Besides, she'd become aware that the whole class was silent and looking at her, including Mr Berry.

'I see that you've decided to join us at last, Clea.' His voice was heavily laced with sarcasm. 'And what, may I ask, was the pressing activity that kept you away from the first ten minutes of the lesson this time?'

As usual she kept her silence and began to blush until he pressed further. 'Well, we're all waiting?'

'I got my period and had to go home to change,' she blurted, leaving the statement floating chaotically around the room.

'Nice one,' said Sarah quietly, with an air punch under the desk that only Clea could see.

Now it was Mr Berry's turn to blush. Clea felt a surge of relief as he swivelled towards the board and continued the lesson, leaving her to slither off the hook.

* * *

When morning classes were over, it was time for lunch.

'I want you to come to a party with me...I'll do your make-up and lend you clothes,' said Sarah, sliding her tray past the soggy vegetables and towards the chips.

Clea reminded her that she was grounded.

'You're always grounded, I've thought of a way around that. You can't spend your whole life cooped up in your bedroom.'

'I s'pose.' Clea was doubtful.

They found a free table to eat at and she listened in disbelief as Sarah revealed her elaborate escape plan.

'I'm not jumping out of a stupid window!' Clea told her when she'd finished.

'It's not like it's that high,' protested Sarah. 'What are you nervous of?'

'I could break my neck, that's what I'm nervous of.'

'Like you're going to. Anyway, you jump off that pole thing all the time when you do your gymnastics.'

'That's different, there's a safety mat underneath me. Besides, what if I get caught?'

'What can they do to you that they haven't done already?' Sarah asked imploringly, blue eyes wide.

Sarah had a serious crush on her big brother's friend and said friend was going to be at the party. Sarah had to be there – it could be her chance to get noticed.

'So, get your brother to take you, easy,' reasoned Clea.

'Don't you think I didn't consider that? He said no already.'

'Amy?' (Sarah's other best friend, who went to a different school.)

'Too pretty...no offence.' None was taken.

'I don't know, Sarah.' Clea spiked some chips and mopped them ponderously in the palette of ketchup on the side of her plate.

III

The principal

The principal had nothing left to throw up, but the dry retching continued.

'Breathe,' she told herself firmly. The recurring dream brought her out of deep sleep more often these days. She inhaled and exhaled deeply, as she did in her yoga classes, and to her relief the retching stopped.

She made her way to the kitchen to fix herself a smoothie. Relining her stomach would help her regain composure. 'Hello, you beautiful little thing,' she crooned, stooping to rub the ears of her old cat, weaving itself fluidly around her legs. The air was thick with the comforting rumble of his purr. 'Hoping for some milk, are you?'

Ten years ago, she would have been fixing herself a whisky and sparking up a cigarette, but a lot had changed since she'd split with her husband.

They'd met on a film; her part – a small, non-speaking cameo. She had been randomly plucked out of a modelling portfolio by a casting agent, and her mother had disapproved. Isobel was only seventeen years old, she saw it as a waste of her academic talent, but she begrudgingly concurred. Mike was the cameraman on the film-set and they'd gone and fallen in love, plop!

She had ignored everyone's advice about taking things a bit more slowly and they had married after just three months of knowing each other.

A year later she had given up modelling to have their first child, going on to have another soon after that. It wasn't easy, in fact it was really bloody difficult, but she had thought they were doing okay.

It was the middle of August when she'd made a trip to the family home in Devon with the kids. Her mother had come to accept that her beautiful daughter had chosen this life and, in her opinion, this rather undeserving man. So, she put her feelings aside and did all that she could to support their relationship.

Knowing how hard two little ones could be on a marriage, she had instructed Isobel to go home and enjoy her husband, *she* would look after the children.

The principal had gone shopping for a new dress, nice underwear – and had raced home to surprise Mike. A sixth sense told her to be quiet when she entered the house her mother had so generously given them as a wedding present, and like a really bad film, she had found him in bed with her younger sister, Sophie. Life as she knew it was over.

English had been her major at university, before the heady side-step into modelling and after the tragedy (as she'd come to think of it) her mother had supported her and the children financially, whilst she finished her degree and completed teacher training.

Her mother had been widowed, leaving her sad but wealthy. She saw the wealth as a great privilege, and wanted her children to pursue careers that were fulfilling and worthwhile, without financial pressure influencing their paths.

When Isobel got a job teaching English at a comprehensive school, she approved, and she was proud.

Increasingly drawn towards working with problem teens and young offenders, Isobel had much success and steadily became a leading authority, so much so that she was headhunted for the position of *principal*, to trial an American model of education at one of the roughest colleges in London.

In just six years she had turned it around and it was now the most successful place for difficult teenagers and young offenders in the country. She had achieved more than she ever could have imagined because inside, where it really mattered, it was a mess and if she stopped, even for a little while, it started to get messier.

Hungrily she gulped the smoothie. The problem was, it

wasn't jus*t a dream.* It was her conscience, reminding her that mistakes longed to be corrected.

IV

Flow

So-called because he was laid back and always *went with the flow* – Flow could draw a caricature of anyone or graffiti a wall in minutes using spray cans or markers; it was his thing – his gift, you could say.

Of all the people Kim knew, Flow was luckiest when it came to family and Kim was luckiest, too, because he got to be a part of it. Flow's mum and dad had always been together, close-knit, as were his nan and grandad. They all lived on the estate, in the block next to Kim's.

Flow's mum and nan made a packet cleaning people's houses, and his dad was a handyman, painting and decorating, mostly. He often took Flow and Kim on jobs with him and gave them a bit of their own work here and there, too.

Biologically speaking, Kim only had his mum, who was on the game. They joked that she must have slept with some superhuman to have come up with Kim and privately, that made her feel a lot better about the fact that Kim had been a surprise, and his heritage a mystery.

Top of her profession in her younger days and highly sought after, she famously slept with royalty and other bigwigs, and made a mint.

Why did she stay on the estate when she had that much money and so many proposals for a different life? Nobody knew. Best guess – maybe her friends on the estate were the closest thing to family she had and she needed to be near them.

'Mum,' Flow yelled from his bedroom. 'Got any wrapping paper?'

He had bought Jackie a new watch, exactly the same as the one he'd smashed. He still didn't understand why she was so upset about it but he did know buying her a new one would make it better.

No reply.

'Muuuum!' he yelled again – still no reply.

He trudged off to find her in front of the telly watching *EastEnders*, feet up, sipping vodka and orange, her favourite tipple after a hard day at work.

She pretended she hadn't noticed him standing in the doorway with his arms crossed.

'Didn't you hear me?'

'Of course I heard you,' she said calmly. 'Wrapping paper is in the second drawer down, left of the kitchen sink along with Sellotape, scissors and curling ribbon.'

Flow knew better than to argue or to ask why she couldn't have simply yelled that information back to him instead of making him walk all the way to the sitting room.

'Thanks,' he muttered, going off to collect the necessary equipment. He hated it when Jackie was cross with him because she withheld sexual favours.

Armed with the parcel, he confidently made his way to Jackie's place in the Glass Block, the tallest building on the estate, and home to his and Kim's crop of grass, cleverly concealed on the roof.

He took the stairs because the lift always stank.

Kim, meanwhile, took his normal route to the park but instead of heading to the playground, he made his way to the benches by the river, where people went when they wanted privacy. He had a date with Sheema, one of the whispering girls from the wall by the paddling pool. Turns out the subject of discussion had been him.

Jackie had acted as go-between, fixing up a date. He had never really considered Sheema in *that way* before but she was pretty, she was friendly – why not?

The Frog Theory

Although he was five minutes early, she was waiting for him, sitting expectantly. He noticed that she smelt of soap and shampoo and they were soon in a long, soft kiss. It was nice.

The window incident

Clea and Sarah had stayed on late at school to attend their self-defence class. Clea was naturally good at anything physical and enjoyed practising the moves. She also shone at acting, in contradiction to her shyness, and was often picked for main parts in school plays (though Hugo detested it). Anything extra-curricular was a good thing, in Clea's eyes, as it meant she could avoid going home for a bit longer.

They were in the sixth form, so it was the equivalent of college, really, but as they had both been there since they were eleven, they still referred to it as 'school'.

Walking to their homes through Parsons Green, they discussed the finer details of Sarah's plan. Tonight, was the night.

Clea had come around to the idea of jumping out of the window. Sarah was right; it made sense to bypass the creaky stairs. She could drop down into the garden, go through the patio doors, then creep along the ground floor of the house and out of the front door when a car went past, to muffle any sound.

'And if you get caught?' said Sarah.

'I'll text gobbledygook letters so it looks like I texted you by mistake, then you don't get into trouble, too.' She rehearsed.

'Yeah...like YAZAGAAAAAAAAAA!'

Sarah made a funny face and laughed.

Clea didn't have to wait long for her mum and Hugo to go to bed. They always retired early in the evening and watched TV or read books, and the other thing they might be doing. Clea didn't even want to think about.

The Frog Theory

She'd left the patio doors in the kitchen unlocked in preparation and had already opened her bedroom window to minimise noise later. She watched the digital clock radio in her room flick to eleven twenty-nine, her heart hammering, and went to check that the sliver of light under their bedroom door had gone – it had. She was ready. She had promised. She wasn't going to let Sarah down.

Shakily, she sat on the window ledge and turned herself around so that she was kneeling on the sill with her bottom pointing towards the garden. She then lowered herself so that she was dangling by her hands. She looked down to the hard, cold patio below, realised how far it was to drop and completely lost her bottle – at the very least she would surely break her legs.

'Muuuuuuuuum!' she cried hoarsely at the top of her lungs. She hung there in terror, scared that she wasn't going to be able to hold on for long enough. She squeezed her eyes shut and clutched the sill as hard as she was able. 'Heeeeeelp!' she yelled.

It was a primal noise that only sheer terror can invoke, prompting her mother and Hugo to leap out of bed. They were in her bedroom in seconds.

Hugo snapped the light on and at first they couldn't see her, despite scanning the room several times. Finally, Hugo's eyes rested upon the two white-knuckled hands clinging onto the sill and they found Clea hanging there.

'What on earth do you think you're doing?' he asked in astonishment.

'Ground me for as long as you want, just get me up,' she said, still not able to open her eyes.

They grabbed an arm each and hauled her onto the sill so that she was able to scramble back in, landing in a crumpled heap on the floor. 'Thank you,' she said, out of breath, holding her heart and looking up at the naked couple. 'Thank you so much.'

*YAZAGAAAAAAAAAA!

Repercussions

Clea had been confined to her bedroom since 'the window incident' and now the smell of Sunday lunch wafted up the stairs – inevitable doom.

'What are you doing in there, masturbating?' said a red-in-the-face Hugo, standing in the doorway of her bedroom with his hands on his hips.

'You're disgusting, Hugo.' She looked at him disdainfully. How could he appear so silently, like a spider?

'I don't want any of your lip,' he said threateningly. 'I can make life extremely miserable for you, do you understand?' He looked at her chest. Instinctively she crossed her arms to cover herself. 'Didn't you hear me calling you for lunch? It's ready.'

She followed him downstairs, sat at the table, and braced herself. 'Well? What have you got to say for yourself, girl? Waking us up like that – gave your mother the most terrible shock to see you hanging there.' He took a healthy slug of red wine and popped a roast potato into his mouth.

She began to explain. 'Don't interrupt. I hadn't finished,' he said through his mouthful of food. They waited while he chewed a bit more. 'What your mother and I want to know is, are you suicidal?'

The idea took her by surprise. She'd never contemplated suicide; would it help to pretend that she had? Probably not.

She started to explain for the second time but didn't get halfway through her sentence before Hugo accused her of interrupting again.

'I told you not to interrupt,' he barked.

'I thought you'd finished.'

'There you go again.' She didn't even bother to look at her mother, she knew she'd get no support from her, she might as well be a piece of tissue paper between them. 'That's the trouble with you,' continued Hugo, 'you never listen. Maybe if you did you'd actually learn a thing or two instead of going through life like a blinkered idiot – and what's wrong with your food? You've hardly touched it. You never eat properly, that's why you look so ill and sallow and the reason your hair's so lank, it's the first thing that happens when someone isn't eating properly.'

In actual fact, though Clea didn't realise it, her complexion was beautiful and her hair was perfectly healthy.

And so it went on, with the following outcome: an hour more of lecturing, during which her mother said nothing. Grounded for six months. Apple crumble (home-made). A slapped face, bruised arm, confinement to her room and a best friend who had disowned her by text because the man of her dreams had got off with someone else at the party and it was all…Clea's… fault.

Dear Diary,

Thank God I have you to talk to, my only friend. I'm locked in the bathroom again after one of my 'turns'. A rising of the blood, dizziness and a feeling of overwhelming panic as life seems to drone past without me. I feel that I have become trapped inside myself, have lost the power of speech, that I am invisible.

Probation

'Let's get breakfast,' said Leigh, one of Kim's on/off flings. She had not been pleased to hear on the grapevine that Kim had started going out with a girl called Sheema, so she'd pulled out all the stops to make him stay with *her* last night. *She* was his girl, even if he didn't realise it yet.

'I can't, I'm helping Flow's old man out on a decorating job today and I'm already late.'

It was as good an excuse as any; he still had time to go home for a shower before his appointment with his probation officer, if he hurried.

Last night was the *last night* he was going to spend with Leigh. It was already a night and a morning too much – she could be persuasive.

'There's no need to lie, I know you're going to see *her*!' Leigh said, pouting.

'If by *her* you mean Sheema, then no, because unlike you she has a job and she's at work. You know? That thing that isn't the dole?'

That shut her up. Leigh couldn't imagine working. It was hard enough just getting through each day as it was.

'Don't go,' she pleaded, grabbing his hand.

'You knew this wasn't serious, Leigh, don't start.' He extracted himself. He hadn't got Sheema into bed yet and he was enjoying the challenge. Besides, if he missed another session with his probation officer, he'd be in serious trouble.

Nick a couple of cars, borrow a bus, graffiti the odd wall and you had to sit and talk about your life every Thursday to some boring sop who didn't have a clue, or go to jail.

Sometimes he considered jail, especially today as he sat in the uninspiring little room.

'For goodness' sake, Kim, don't you care about your future? You've missed more than six appointments,' his probation officer was saying.

'I was working,' he said defensively.

'I can't keep protecting you.'

Kim eyed the mousy, middle-aged woman as she nervously worked out what to say next. 'You don't seem to realise that I'm on your side,' she said.

'On my back, more like,' interrupted Kim. Defensive behaviour got you further with these people.

'And in return,' she continued, after a pause, 'when you do turn up you're defensive, uncooperative and rude, which makes me wonder why I bother.'

'So you can go to bed with your halo glowing,' he answered.

Something about her change of countenance made him regret his words a little.

'Well, I was going to suggest a special college, but with an attitude like that...'

'What do you mean, *special college*, do you think I'm thick or something?' His temper flared, he was the one being patronised now.

'I know you're not *thick*, as you put it, Kim – managing to get eight GCSEs, all above C-average when you hardly ever went to school shows quite the opposite.'

Kim shrugged – he had been surprised, too. 'What's this... *College*, then?' he said, after a moment's contemplation.

Catching the train

The principal took the Tube to and from work, getting on at Sloane Square, which was near her home off the Kings Road. She enjoyed the journey, it gave her the chance to read the news, prepare, relax – as long as she left obscenely early, otherwise the carriage would be jam-packed.

Lately, she couldn't help noticing a man getting on the same carriage as her, most days, at South Kensington. She observed that he was in his late forties, always in a smart suit, and wore a gold band on his wedding ring finger. She wasn't sure, but it seemed like he was surreptitiously checking her out. She supposed he was what you would call attractive, if you were looking for a man, which she definitely *was not*, especially one that was married.

The principal was used to being looked at and it hadn't bothered her up until now. Maybe it was the fact that his attention didn't strike her as altogether unpleasant? He caught her eye and smiled a little, as if he were confused about something. She didn't respond – she went back to the news, crossing her long legs.

Gossiping girls

'You've been seeing Leigh, you bastard!' Sheema accused, as soon as she opened the door to Kim, keeping him in the hallway.

'Who told you that?' he asked, caught unawares.

'Does it matter?'

Jackie was such a good friend to have filled her in.

'It matters to me.'

'She's a fucking slapper, Kim. There's more bleach in her hair than what's down my toilet.' Her eyes began to brim. 'Get out!' she yelled, angrily wiping her hand across her face; tears had not been in the plan.

She'd let him stew for a week, then think about taking him back if he grovelled hard enough. She put his infidelity down to the fact that she, herself, had not slept with him yet and besides, Leigh had probably thrown herself at him, the cheap slut.

Ousted, Kim digested the information. He knew that it must have been Jackie who'd opened her mouth to Sheema and he also knew that he should let it go, because purposely messing up people's lives was Jackie's hobby, yet he found himself at the Glass Block knocking on her door.

Jackie's mum answered, Jackie was in.

'You told Sheema I was still seeing Leigh, didn't you?' Kim asked as soon as they were in the privacy of Jackie's bedroom, unable to conceal his anger.

Jackie went red and played nervously with her cigarette packet. Even though it wasn't done to grass, and Flow had said there was nothing in it, seeing Sheema all lovey-dovey had been getting on her nerves so she'd got her pin out and burst her bubble. She deserved it, the smug cow.

'I didn't say anything. Leigh was mouthing off to everyone that she was going out with you, they all heard, not just me.'

'Mouthing off to who? Leigh doesn't know anyone from our estate, so who was she mouthing off to? No one, that's who.'

'I'm sorry,' she found herself saying, faltering, looking at the floor. Kim's presence was powerful and being alone with him now, she felt like he could see right through her.

'Why would you do that? Upset your mate for no reason?' he asked, confused.

'I told you, I didn't,' she said. 'And if I did it wasn't on purpose. Anyway, you can make it up to her and she'll take you back, honest she will, I know her.'

The Frog Theory

'I don't want to make it up to her.' His temper was gone now. He knew that whatever he said would go straight back to Sheema and he wasn't going to grovel his way back into her life. He didn't want a girlfriend holding him back, being a pain in the arse, anyway.

'Then maybe I could make it up to you?' Jackie said, lying back on the bed, stretching out her neat figure for him to appreciate. He took in her body language. Was his best mate's girlfriend honestly expecting him to accept an offer like that?

'Not in a million years,' he said, embarrassed and disgusted. 'You don't deserve Flow. He'll see through you one day and when he does I'll be there to help him celebrate.'

'Your loss!' she shouted after him as he slammed her bedroom door.

The fight

That evening at the playground there was no sign of anyone apart from Paula, who was sitting on the wall, idly swinging her legs as Kim made his way over.

'Got caught out, then?' she said with a friendly chuckle, lighting a cigarette for him as he sat next to her. She treasured these moments of camaraderie with the boys. 'Never mind, love.'

'Bad news travels fast,' said Kim, taking the lit cigarette from her. 'Because unlike you, some people can't keep their mouths shut.'

'And some people just can't keep their dick in their trousers,' Paula quipped back with a sideways glance full of glee, seeing whether he'd take the bait and tease her back.

Nobody gets it out for you, though, he thought, but he didn't say that because it was the kind of comment that would make her cry in the dark late at night and he didn't want to hurt her, so instead he drew in a long lug of smoke. 'Just watch your back, will ya?' she advised. She had a soft spot for Kim.

Jackie had told her there was a lot of 'shit' going down, which meant some new drama, probably of Jackie's own twisted making, was about to unfold. She had always been a devious troublemaker and got off on other people's pain, it was her nature.

Paula didn't question their friendship, built out of habit and loyalty, she simply accepted Jackie for all that she was.

The playground was beginning to fill with people now, one of whom was Leigh. Her finest asset was her looks. She was wearing a figure-hugging red smocked stretchy dress that

The Frog Theory

was more like a long vest top, and she clearly wore no bra underneath.

'Here comes the tart!' Paula said loudly enough for everyone to hear.

Not put off, Leigh made directly for them.

'Hi stranger,' Leigh said to Kim, completely ignoring Paula, fixing him with a look that meant one thing.

Kim shifted uncomfortably, aware of Paula watching. 'I want to talk,' she continued, her lips pleasantly glossed and inviting, eyes glittering slightly with whatever she had taken.

'Not here,' said Kim, steering her off towards the benches by the river.

Once they were alone, Leigh put a condom into his hand.

'I'm horny as hell.' She French kissed him passionately and pulled him into the trees.

'I thought you wanted to talk,' he said breathlessly between kisses, caught in the moment, hungrily kissing her back.

'Changed my mind.' She pulled the front of her dress down to expose her chest and released Kim from his jeans. She wiggled the little dress up from the bottom, so that it was nothing more than a wide belt.

Kim lifted her up so that she could wrap her legs around him, using the tree to support her, the bulk of the dress the only thing stopping the skin on her back from being ripped to shreds while they were lost in their world.

She was high on amphetamine and vodka and lust, taken away to the place that made her forget mortality; nothing in life was better than these moments, she lived for them, especially when they were with Kim. Afterwards they panted, exhausted and dizzy. As the high passed, all Kim wanted was to push her away. He snapped the condom off and held it up to check it. His heart skipped.

'It broke,' he said in amazement.

'No big deal, I'll go for the morning-after pill tomorrow.'

She said it like she did that all the time so he didn't give it a second thought.

'I've got to go.' He threw the condom into the bushes and zipped himself up.

'That's okay, I'll go with you. I haven't got anything else to do,' she said, ignoring his brush off.

'I've got some business to sort out.'

'What sort of business?' She tried to take his hand.

'Puff.'

'I want to come with you,' she whinged, straightening her dress, ready to follow him anywhere.

That was the trouble with Leigh, she could outdo most women when it came to looks and she was magnetic when she wanted sex, but the rest of the time her neediness was like a spinning vortex. What he needed now was a pint and a game of pool with Flow; he wondered where he was.

He went to the pub on the bridge to clean himself up in the loos then made his way back to the playground. Thankfully, Leigh had made herself scarce, but Sheema was sitting on the wall with Paula.

'You'll catch summink, the way you carry on,' she sniped as he passed by on his way over to Pat and Ryan.

He looked around yet again for Flow and finally saw him walking purposefully in his direction, closely followed by Jackie who had her arms crossed, mouth set in a tight line. Instead of greeting Kim as he usually did, he punched him square in the face.

'Woah.' Kim held his jaw and staggered backwards. 'What the fuck's up with you?'

Flow gave him another punch that put him on the ground. 'What's this about?' Kim was bewildered, he had never hit Flow and he had no intention of doing so now.

'I never thought you'd sink so fucking low.' Flow scorned, pulling him up by the collars so that only the tips of his feet were touching the ground and he had partially disappeared into his shirt.

'Flow,' said Kim in bemusement, 'what do you think I've done?' he hung in Flow's grip like a wounded puppy, willingly subservient, whilst Flow scrutinised his expression for the tiniest tell that would give him away.

There was none. Either Jackie was exceptional at lying or Kim didn't consider himself out of order.

'You tried to get hold of Jackie,' Flow said through clenched teeth.

There was a moment while it sank in.

'Like fuck I did,' Kim sneered, smacking Flow's hands away from him so that he stood fully on his feet once more, his shirt relocating somewhere around his neck. He wasn't going to show Flow up by saying Jackie had been the one to try it on with him so he walked off, blood dripping down his front.

'That's it, Kim, walk off like you always do,' shouted Sheema. 'You fucking prick!'

Job interview

Kim looked at his reflection in the bathroom mirror. His eye was beginning to go down now and his nose definitely wasn't broken.

Ryan had put him and their friend Pat up for a building job in the New Forest and he didn't want to look like he'd done a couple of rounds with Lennox Lewis.

He was grateful to Ryan for coming up with the idea because a couple of weeks away were exactly what he needed right about now. It was an example of how Ryan could be an exceptionally good and thoughtful mate at times.

'Not too bashed up, then,' said Ryan, when he opened the door to him. 'What was the story there?'

'Misunderstanding,' answered Kim.

'Suit yourself if you don't want to talk about it. The old man's in the kitchen.'

Kim walked confidently through to find Mick sitting at the table.

'You've grown. Haven't seen you since you was a nipper.'

'Ryan said you might have some work for me.'

Kim ignored the silly comment. Of course he'd grown and Mick *had* seen him, plenty of times, he could be odd like that.

'Yeah, I've got some work, building camping conveniences.'

Mick looked Kim up and down. Half the kids on the estate were on drugs and would nick what they could and scarper as soon as your back was turned. 'Are you a drug user?'

'What?' Kim wasn't sure whether he had heard correctly.

'You know, on the old wacky backy?'

'Oh, that. Not me, mate.'

'Where d'ya get the black eye?'

Ryan walked in and flicked the kettle on.

'Flow's bird made out he was trying to shag it.'

Ryan always knew the score.

'And was he?' Mick was hooked on the story for a moment.

'Nah.' Ryan exchanged a glance with Kim. 'Tea?' he asked, waving a box of PG Tips. The interview was apparently over – they would be leaving in the morning.

Mick drove them to the New Forest in his sizable van, loaded up with tents and tools. As they got further away from London, Kim watched the road passing by and tried to shake the memory of the fight from his mind. It scared him that he may have lost the only link to something that felt like family he possessed. He had never fallen out with Flow and it was hurtful at a core level, but there was nothing to be done. He had not touched Jackie, and if Ryan could work it out, Flow could work it out.

'Do you think they'll be any nice birds in the New Forest?' said Pat.

'You wouldn't be able to pull a nice bird even if you had one sitting in a shopping trolley,' said Ryan.

Pat tried to work out a retaliation and failed. Mick chipped in and slowly the banter going back and forth took Kim's mind away from himself.

The pitching of the tents had the men cracking up with laughter, and a few pints at the pub knocked off any remaining sharp edges for them all.

The principal

'I thought we could do something today, Mum,' her daughter said nervously.

'Like what, darling?' The principal took a sip of her coffee, trying not to think about how much Emily looked like her father, Mike. She hated it when her children came home from boarding school. Thankfully, her son stayed in bed in the mornings but her daughter would hang around like she wanted something.

'Well…' said Emily, 'like anything. I could go to the college with you and help?'

'No,' said her mother more abruptly than she meant to, ignoring the fact that Emily was fighting back tears.

The dream had woken her yet again last night. Always the same – Mike lying in a coffin, opening his eyes and sitting up. 'What about Matilda? Couldn't you go somewhere with her today?' she said more gently. Matilda was one of Emily's best friends.

'I want to go somewhere with you,' she shouted. 'You're always too busy with that…that fucking college!'

'I don't think swearing's going to help anything,' said the principal, calmly.

'Fuck fuck fuck fuck fuck!' Emily chanted defiantly.

The principal got up to leave.

'Hopefully when I come home you'll be in a better mood,' she said, leaving the rest of her coffee. She felt like she was going to throw up, and hurried from the house.

Chuck me a rope

As usual, her mum and Hugo had made themselves scarce and Clea was left alone, bored and frustrated. She paced the house, wondering what to do with herself and spotted Hugo's packet of cigarettes on the side table in the sitting room. She took one out of the packet then helped herself to a large glass of red wine from the wine box in the kitchen and went up to her bedroom, where she leant out of the window.

Tentatively, she took some smoke in and didn't even cough, it was all right! She breathed in the warm night air with the smoke, then blew it out gently. She took a big gulp of the red wine, holding it in her mouth for a while to get the flavour before she swallowed it.

The moon was out and she could hear the distant voices of people enjoying themselves. She imagined the bars brimming, parties heaving, romantic dinners being eaten. She could even see some people drinking champagne in a roof garden not far away and she wanted to shout, *Over here! Chuck me a rope.*

In theory, she could just leave home. She was eighteen. But where would she go? Hugo may be a bastard and her mother may be a fence sitter but they were the only family she had.

Besides, she had this niggling feeling that somehow it was her fault they treated her the way they did. It was stupid, and nobody would understand, but she was sure there was some reason for it, otherwise why didn't her mother stick up for her?

Dear Diary,
Me again, in a state as usual. I've got these pills from the doctor, now, though, they calm me down. It says to take one but I have taken two with a massive glass of wine, waiting for better feelings to kick in. I told Hugo I had one of my migraines and was taking a bath. He doesn't care, I think he's relieved not to be in the same room as me for a while, happy watching his beloved TV in bed...

New Forest

The break and change of scene were doing Kim good. Sun, fresh air, physical labour, it kept his mind off other things. A week in, he was interested to see how Mick ran the job – another week and they would be done; shower blocks and utility room, ran like clockwork, he made it look easy.

In the evenings they would go to the local pub for dinner and a couple of pints, have a bit of a laugh. There were plenty

The Frog Theory

of holidaymakers around and everyone was out to have a good time, so it caught Kim off-guard to find Jackie standing in front of him, an unwelcome reminder of all he had left at home.

'What the fuck do *you* want?' he said rudely, stopping in his tracks. The pub beckoned.

'Well thanks a lot,' said Jackie, pouting. 'I came to say I was sorry about the fight and the misunderstanding and…it's not exactly around the corner so a little appreciation might be nice.'

'Misunderstanding?' said Kim, incredulously.

Jackie held her ground. 'Flow asked if we'd been alone in my bedroom and you tell me what I was meant to say?' She raised her hands helplessly to emphasise her point. 'We didn't have anything to hide so I said yes and he jumped to incorrect conclusions.'

'You tried to get off with me.'

'That never crossed my mind, I don't know what made you think that,' said Jackie, brushing it off. 'Tell Flow it was a misunderstanding when you come back to London, he really wants to make up. We've got everything worked out now, be a shame to spoil it all, I don't want him kicking off again…I didn't want him to hit you but there was nothing I could do about it.' Kim said nothing so she carried on. 'I love Flow but he has a temper, you just don't see it, he scares me. Sometimes I think he's going to hit *me*.'

'I don't believe you, Jackie,' said Kim, seething that she could imply Flow was threatening. 'I've known Flow since he was a kid and there's never been a violent bone in his body.'

'You don't see him when we're alone, he's different, he gets jealous…tell him it was a misunderstanding.'

'You're making him out to be some sort of monster when the only reason he hit me is because *you* told him I tried it on, that's the truth but you have to twist everything.'

'Kim, please…tell him it was a misunderstanding…then we can all go back to normal and forget it.'

'I'm telling him nothing, you're the one who lies…get out of it yourself, like you always do.'

Saying no to her meant risking the most important friendship in his life but he wasn't going to lie. He got about three inches from her face and lowered his voice menacingly. 'I said it before, Jackie, and I'll say it again. Flow will see through you in his own good time.'

She bit her lip with rage.

'I never tried to get off with you, Kim, you just think you're God's gift and by the way...I have a bit of information that might interest you.' She paused for dramatic effect. 'Leigh's pregnant, and she's telling everyone it's yours.' She watched with satisfaction as his face fell, before stalking off.

Later, in Ryan's tent

'What...in this world...could possibly have taken you so long?'

'I didn't want to make it obvious, did I? I stayed drinking with the lads so they wouldn't suspect.'

He didn't mention that he'd also been fixing up a date with a girl for the following night.

'You could have said you were ill or something, I've been stuck in this sodding tent all night waiting for you. And you owe me the train fare, by the way.' She turned her back and crossed her arms.

'How could I say I was ill when I was fine all day? They'd bust me for sure...Jackie, I was only thinking of you, babe...I was bored shitless, watching the clock all night – waiting for last orders.'

'Really?' she said, turning slightly.

'Really...and considering you tried to get hold of Kim, I think I'm the one who should be annoyed here, don't you?'

'I didn't try to get hold of Kim, how many times have I got to say? That bloke just can't get it into his head that not every girl in the world...'

'Come here,' interrupted Ryan, pulling her towards him. He felt bad on Flow but Flow wasn't going to find out, and it had been Jackie who had come onto him a couple of months back.

The party

Every year, at the end of the summer, Flow's nan hired out the British Legion and threw a party for her birthday. Flow and Kim had been to them every year of their lives, as had most of the kids on the estate. It was an institution.

Kim planned to be there. He was pretty sure that if he bought Flow a drink as usual, their problems would get resolved.

He counted his cash from the New Forest job and looked around for an envelope, not really expecting to find one. (His mum didn't write many letters.) Instead, he put a substantial wad of notes in an old shopping bag with Leigh's name written on in marker pen and scrawled – *from Kim*.

Absentmindedly, he traced the scar on the side of his head, left when he had been knocked unconscious on a bicycle pedal at the age of seven, by one of his mum's clients. He often ran his hand over it.

He shoved the bag containing the money through Leigh's letter box and made his way to the party.

Ordinarily, Flow's nan would have been at the party first to welcome everyone but this year she was taking an unexpected diversion from the norm. She had been asked for a favour by one of her clients, *Hugo*. Would she watch his stepdaughter while they went to an evening seminar, to do with Hugo's work? Clea was eighteen, for goodness' sake, why did she need *watching*?

She didn't like Hugo, or the way he spoke to Clea – a shy, unconfident thing. She had seen a bruise on her once and had almost said something but she had learnt to keep her nose out of other people's business, especially those hoity-toity types.

The house was usually empty when she went in to clean with her daughter anyway, so she let it pass and now, rather than asking him why he thought Clea should be *watched*, she said *yes*, as long as they didn't mind her being dragged to a seventieth birthday party.

They didn't mind.

'Thank you for this, Elsie. Here's the delinquent girl,' said Hugo, pushing poor Clea forward.

'Hi Elsie,' said Clea shyly.

'Back by ten,' Hugo stipulated.

'Not a minute over,' promised Elsie. She felt goose bumps climb her back and instinctively ushered Clea down the path and out of the gate without further chat.

The British Legion wasn't very far, they were travelling on foot.

'I hope you're going to have a good time, love.'

Elsie got the feeling Hugo wouldn't like the idea of Clea having a good time at all.

'Anything's got to be better than that house!'

Guilt consumed Clea as soon as the unexpected words tumbled out, and she blushed deeply, hiding once more beneath her hair.

'You can say what you like to me, my darling, I'll say nothing to nobody, right?' She tried to give her a reassuring look but it was impossible to make eye contact under that fringe. 'I didn't tell your lot,' she pushed on, 'but it's my birthday and there's plenty of young folk there…it'll be quite a do.'

'Oh!' Said Clea. 'I didn't realise…happy birthday, I'm sorry I…didn't want to cause any bother…' she trailed off.

'Bother? How could a gorgeous girl like you be a bother?' She gently scolded, linking her arm. Her unexpected kindness lifted Clea and she began to cheer up. Maybe the night wasn't going to be so bad after all.

* * *

The Frog Theory

Flow was at the bar with Jackie, who looked Kim straight in the eye as he approached, a little smile playing just for him. He felt a surge of hate rise in his chest.

'Wanna go and powder your nose, Jacks?' Flow pointedly suggested. He wanted to speak to Kim alone, eager to make amends. Falling out with his best mate had been traumatic. 'So, how've you been?'

Kim felt his whole self rest now that he knew for sure things were going to be okay.

'I'll be better for a pint.' He tried to catch the barman's eye.

'I've heard your news,' said Flow, when Kim had got the drinks in. 'Leigh up the duff and Sheema's spitting nails.' Kim grimaced and took a few gulps of his lager.

'Thanks for the recap.'

'About the fight,' Flow began awkwardly. 'I was out of order...I owe you an apology.'

'Sure,' said Kim, nodding. 'Forget it.'

'Yeah, well...' he continued, 'I feel gutted about it, going off like that, but Jackie finally told me what really happened and we've sorted things.'

'Good...I'm glad.' He wondered what shit Jackie had filled his head with this time.

'Yeah...we've decided to get married.'

'Pttttttttttter!' Kim unintentionally spat a fountain of beer across the bar. 'Since when?'

'Well...since she asked me.' Flow laughed nervously, looking at the mess.

'Congratulations,' muttered Kim, mopping half-heartedly with a beer mat. 'Any idea when?'

'Oh...you know, we're not in a hurry. I mean...Well, a couple of years or something. We haven't really thought it through.'

The barman came over with a proper cloth and began to clean up briskly. They both watched, grateful for the distraction.

'Went down the wrong way,' explained Kim to the barman, by way of apology.

'Happens,' the barman replied pleasantly, already done and pulling another drink.

Jackie returned and Flow gave her a kiss.

'You heard our news, then?' She nestled into the crook of Flow's arm.

'Sure did.' Kim fixed a smile on his face. 'Sure did.' He drained the last of his beer in a single long swallow, beckoning the barman for a refill.

'Ay up, what's this?' Jackie eyed Elsie, steering someone towards them.

'This is Clea,' Elsie began. 'And I want you to look after her as a personal favour to me.' She grabbed Flow's cheeks and gave him a kiss. 'Isn't he lovely? My youngest grandson and just look at the size of him.' After she had finished with Flow, she grabbed Kim's cheeks, introducing him too, then ruffled his hair as if he were a small child, although she could hardly reach his head. 'Jackie.' She acknowledged politely, her face suddenly less friendly.

'Hap-pee birthday, Nan!' said Flow, picking her up and swinging her around as she squealed and protested.

'Happy birthday, Elsie,' said Kim, when Flow had finally put her down. 'What are you drinking?'

'Don't worry, my love, I'll sort myself out,' she said, as various friends began to descend upon her. 'Just look after Clea for me,' she said sternly, leaving them to it.

Kim looked Clea up and down. She was medium height and dying of embarrassment. She had long, blondish hair, which was covering most of her face, and she was wearing a shapeless dress, which didn't give any clue as to what her figure might be like.

'You look like Cousin Itt off *The Munsters* under all that hair,' said Kim, as an ill-chosen icebreaker.

'I think you'll find that Cousin Itt featured in *The Addams Family*, actually,' she replied tartly.

The Frog Theory

La-di-da! thought Kim, Jackie and Flow simultaneously.

'He was only kidding,' said Flow, trying to save the day. 'Can I get you a drink?'

'Sauvignon blanc, please,' said Clea, without thinking much. It was the only white wine she had heard of.

'Errrrr...' said Flow, exchanging glances with Kim. 'I'm not sure they'll *feature* any of that at this bar! It's a white wine, isn't it?'

'Actually, I'll have whatever you're drinking,' she said, eager to get the attention away from herself as soon as possible.

'A pint of lager?'

'No...not that.' She looked at Jackie's drink. 'What are you drinking?' she asked shyly, in a glazed millisecond taking in Jackie's dark good looks and beautifully fitted top and skirt combo, complementing her curvy, compact figure. Her bra strap was showing and it was red. Clea had never owned red underwear.

'Vodka-lemonade,' said Jackie, still looking her up and down.

'I'll have one of those, please,' she said, blushing again as Flow beckoned for the barman.

They stood in embarrassed silence. Clea stared downwards, taking in Jackie's shapely legs; black strappy high sandals wrapped around neat feet, sporting immaculately polished red toenails. Flow's well-worn trainers that looked loved and comfortable below some sort of dark trousers.

'So...what brings you here?' asked Jackie at last. Clea looked up, flicking her hair out of her face.

Kim couldn't work out whether she was beautiful or ugly. She had the kind of looks that needed a second opinion.

'My mum and stepdad asked Elsie to keep an eye on me because they didn't want me in the house on my own. I'm grounded,' she finished lamely, retreating behind her hair.

Flow handed the vodka and lemonade under the blond mop and she reached for it gratefully.

'What did you get grounded for?' asked Kim, intrigued.

'For trying to jump out of my bedroom window,' she said, so shyly and quietly that they only just heard her.

'Trying?' questioned Kim – this was getting better.

'Lemming!' said Jackie under her breath.

'I was meant to be going to a party,' said Clea, a little more loudly,

'Why didn't you use the front door?' asked Kim, teasing her now but not unkindly. 'It's what most people do, you know? Much safer and more conventional than jumping out of a window.'

'I'm aware of how most people come and go from their houses,' said Clea testily, flicking her hair out of her face again and fixing Kim with a stare that said don't mess with me. 'It's just that I wasn't meant to be going out, stupid!'

Flow and Jackie stifled giggles; it was a first for a girl not to respond to Kim's charms and…stupid? What kind of insult was that?

Jackie wished Paula would hurry up and get there; Paula hated snobs and would give *La-di-da* a run for her money.

Kim suppressed a laugh, too, and resolved to stop teasing. Clea obviously didn't understand that it was their way of connecting with her and he didn't want to be disrespectful to Elsie, who had trusted them. Besides, he had made enough girls cry lately.

'Well, if I jumped out of my bedroom window I'd end up in a morgue,' he said.

'Are your parents strict too?' asked Clea, in surprise.

'No. We live on the seventh floor of Sullivan Court,' said Kim, taking it for granted that Clea would have heard of the biggest council estate in Fulham. She hadn't. But she got the joke and smiled, won over just a little.

She had finished her drink more quickly than she intended and thought another one would be nice but she didn't have any money. 'Besides, you did end up at a party,' said Kim, 'in the end.' He reached across Clea as he spoke, beckoning for the barman, brushing her hand by mistake as he did so. He

The Frog Theory

ordered another vodka and lemonade. 'A good one, too,' he said, handing her the fresh drink.

'Dance,' said Flow, pulling Jackie onto the dance floor. The lights had been dimmed and it was a relief for Clea, who didn't feel so exposed now.

'Shall we?' Kim offered. It was all pretty low-key middle of the road stuff that traversed the age groups. Clea was comfortable dancing. Like the acting, it was in contradiction to her shyness and the low light meant she could totally relax. Nothing flashy or anything, she just had rhythm and enjoyed the beats – she didn't get to hear much music at home.

Jackie bristled to see Clea getting so much attention from Kim, and she caught Flow stealing a few glances at her, too. She'd had enough of *La-di-da* stealing the spotlight so when Elsie came over and asked whether Kim could walk Clea home to meet her ten o'clock curfew, she was only too pleased to say goodbye to the girl.

As soon as they were alone a strange silence descended upon them. She was too prickly, too posh and too weird, thought Kim, and the sooner he got back to the party, the better.

'So...' said Clea eventually, struggling to keep up with his long strides. 'Do you live with your mum and dad?'

'Yep,' lied Kim.

'Does Elsie live on the same estate?'

'Yep,' said Kim.

'Do you have any brothers and sisters?' she asked.

'Look, what are you, a trainee journalist or detective or something?' he said, stopping in his tracks, swivelling to face her.

'I was trying to be friendly,' said Clea, stopping too.

'Well...okay,' said Kim, awkwardly. He wasn't really keen to go into the details of his home life – but more unsettling was that being near her gave him a physical buzz. It had happened when he'd accidentally brushed her hand at the bar and quite a lot when they had been dancing, and if this was the same strange chemistry at work that enabled Jackie to control Flow, he didn't want anything more to do with it.

'Well, I know you've got a front door you're able to walk in and out of,' quipped Clea, hoping to lighten him up a little.

He grunted noncommittally in reply and they walked on in silence until she stopped in front of a smart terraced house.

'This is where I live,' she announced.

Kim looked it up and down. He recognised it. He and Flow had helped on a decorating job nearby and they had seen a man coming and going, getting in and out of a Porsche.

'It's nicer than my place,' he said, turning on his heel. 'See you around,' he called, with a dismissive wave over his shoulder.

'See you around,' whispered Clea with a single windscreen wipe of a wave at his fast departing back.

Once in her room she began to replay the evening in her mind. She lay on her bed, fully dressed, on top of the bedclothes, with her hands locked behind her head. A little smile played on her face. She had been out! True, she would probably never see any of them again and Kim couldn't wait to get away from her, but she had tasted friendship and freedom and vodka-lemonade, and it had been wonderful.

Inside Clea's house

Ever since the party a tension, worse than usual, had been building. It was as though the lasting high Clea had experienced from the event had made her glow and the light was causing her stepfather pain.

She didn't understand why it was bothering him so much. Knowing he was discussing it with her mother, she lay with her ear to the floor of her bedroom so that she could just about hear what was being said in the kitchen below.

'Because,' he was saying, 'she was with those young skanks from the council estate. She was probably taking drugs and fornicating. It's how it happens, you know, the slippery slope, and it's our *responsibility* to find out what went on.'

Hugo called her downstairs and began to question her more

The Frog Theory

about the party, demanding every detail, even though Clea had been through it many times. He wanted to know exactly who had been there, who had walked her home, what they had talked about, whether she had drunk alcohol, and so on and so forth, and it was wearing her out.

'Yes, I had vodka and lemonade – so what? I'm eighteen, it's legal and why *shouldn't* I go out for a good time now and again?' she said, exasperated.

Whack! It was harder than usual because he had used one of his heavy brogues as a weapon, swinging the heel heavily against the side of her head.

'You insubordinate *bitch!*' The words left his mouth like well-aimed bullets made of hate and rage.

Flow was on his way to the corner shop to get a pint of milk for his mum when Clea came hurtling out of nowhere and nearly knocked him over.

'Sorry,' she mumbled.

'It's you,' said Flow, not remembering her name but knowing it was something weird.

Clea looked at him through her hair, it was one of the guys from Elsie's party, the nice one who'd bought her a drink at the beginning. 'Are you all right?' he asked, full of concern. He could tell she'd been crying and her lip was split.

'Not really,' she said, shaking. 'My stepdad lost it…' She looked as if she was going to collapse any minute, so he made her sit on a garden wall.

Clea was too unsteady to stand again so he told her to wait on the wall for him while he completed his mission for milk, then steered her back towards his place for a cup of sweet tea, which he knew was the best thing for shock.

Kim had been knocked out by one of his mum's clients on a bicycle pedal once, when they were seven. Kim's mum had carried him over to their place in her arms, hysterical, wearing nothing more than a pair of knickers, saying she couldn't take Kim to hospital because they'd send him into care.

Flow's mum had wrapped her in a dressing gown and had given her sweet tea; told Flow to stay in his room. *She* had been the one to take Kim to the hospital. Later on, Flow's mum and dad had spoken to Kim's mum in the kitchen for hours, with the door shut.

'Drink this,' said Flow, handing Clea the cup of sweet tea. She did and she felt much better.

'Thanks,' she said. 'I'm really sorry.'

'Sorry that some idiot smashed you up? What's the matter with ya?' He peered under her hair to see whether he could coax a smile. 'Tell you what, why don't you come out with us, Friday night?'

'I don't think your friends liked me that much,' said Clea. 'Besides, what about my lip?'

'Lip, shmip,' said Flow dismissively. 'It's not that bad and it won't even show by the weekend, you'll see.' What was he thinking? How was he going to get Jackie out of the way? She would go mad.

These were puzzles for later.

Flow's dilemma

Kim was surprised to find Flow on his doorstep asking nervously for a favour. Could he go to Clea's house to get her phone number and say he needed to make their night out another time?

Jackie's mum was throwing a family get-together to celebrate the engagement this Friday – Jackie had taken it for granted he would be there and no excuse was going to get him out of it.

Kim was surprised and pleased that Flow was showing an interest in any woman other than Jackie, even if it *was* prickly posh *La-di-da*, so he was more than happy to do it.

'Wouldn't want her to think you stood her up.' He smirked. Flow said that it wasn't like that but they both knew that it *was* like that.

'There's something about Clea and I thought...well, doesn't

The Frog Theory

matter what I thought. I just have to work out what to do – it's bad timing with the engagement thing and all.'

Maybe Flow was being paranoid but he'd begun to suspect that Jackie was not all that she seemed. He had seen a call from Ryan come in which Jackie had sent to answerphone and she had told him it was Paula. He was pretty sure some texts had come in, too.

His interest in Clea had shown him that Jackie might not be the be all and end all after all. In fact, everything about his relationship with Jackie was beginning to feel a little bit wrong.

It was a worry.

The frog theory

It was unusual for Clea to lie to her mother and Hugo and she thought that she would feel guilty. Tonight, however, she felt nothing but excitement. The cover story was that she was going to a lecture with Sarah. It was a risk, but it was unlikely Sarah was going to phone the house, since the many attempts to make up after the window incident had been ignored.

She had bathed and shaved her legs, washed and dried her hair and put her underwear on. Now she was in a panic because she didn't know what to wear. As she thumbed through her scanty wardrobe she realised, with a sick jolt, that the selection of shapeless clothes had all been chosen to stop Hugo leering at her figure.

Now, for the first time in her life, she actually wanted to look attractive. She picked out a dark blue wool coat, which was belted and hung just above the knee. She tried it on with some longish boots and it looked pretty good – showed off her legs. All she needed now was something to go underneath, but before she had the chance to address that problem, the doorbell rang, half an hour earlier than expected.

Kim had decided to pop in on Clea to tell her the change of plan on the way to the off-licence. Ryan's dad was away on another job so he, Ryan and Paula were going to get some beers and go for a smoke at Ryan's place before the pub tonight.

As soon as the bell rang Clea took the stairs like a bounding ostrich, two at a time, to get there before her mum and Hugo did. Phew! She made it, yelled her goodbye and slammed the front door behind her, a little harder than she meant.

The Frog Theory

'Where's Flow?' she asked, taken aback at seeing Kim.

'He couldn't make it...family reunion,' he improvised. 'Said he was sorry and would come 'round soon, asked me to get your number.'

'So, what am I meant to do now?'

'I don't know,' said Kim nonchalantly, unable to look her in the face in case the chemistry got him again.

'What's the hold up?' called Ryan from the gate, eager to inspect whatever girl Kim had picked up.

'I can't go back in,' said Clea in a hushed whisper.

Reluctantly he looked at her properly and found that he couldn't stop. He took in her fair skin with a sprinkling of little freckles and her big amber eyes; she was definitely beautiful, rather than ugly.

'Come on then,' he said impatiently, taking it for granted that she would follow.

They arrived at Ryan's place on the estate. Paula was pretty unfortunate looking but she had nice eyes and nice hair, thought Clea. Ryan wasn't bad looking and talked a lot. He kept staring at her legs, which didn't make her feel sick the way it did when Hugo looked at them.

Kim was a mystery. He had been defensive with her to the point of rudeness so far, and she felt hurt and insulted by it. He was obviously well liked and well respected by his friends, though. She noticed Paula had a major crush on him.

To look at, he was amazing – tall, dark and the greenest eyes, but it was more than physical, he radiated a calm presence and strength of spirit.

'Smoke?' said Ryan, passing Clea a joint. She took a few drags without coughing (she was proud of that) thanked him and passed it back.

'For fuck's sake,' said Paula. 'You were meant to pass it to me.'

'I beg your pardon?' said Clea, politely.

'The puff.' Paula raised her eyes to heaven, she hated it when Kim brought his girlfriends out with him. 'It goes this way.'

'I'm sorry,' said Clea. 'I didn't mean to be impolite, I didn't know it worked like that.' She looked at the floor while an uncomfortable silence surrounded them, feeling Paula's glare penetrate her like a couple of death rays.

'Where's the loo, please?' Clea asked Ryan. She didn't actually need to go but it was boiling in Ryan's place with the heating on and she needed to open her coat for a little while to cool off mentally and physically.

As soon as she'd left the room Paula asked Kim what he was doing with a snob.

'I'm not *with* her,' he said, searching his mind for a viable explanation. 'Elsie asked me if I'd take her out one night, that's all.'

'Hasn't she got her own friends?'

'I don't fucking know, ask her,' he said aggressively, to stop her questions.

'What's your sort doing with the likes of us?' Paula confronted Clea as soon as she returned. 'Shouldn't you be haw-hawing outside the White Horse with the rest of them?'

'Leave it,' said Ryan. 'She isn't doing you any harm.' He'd noticed her nice legs and wouldn't mind a bit if Kim wasn't interested. He had soon recognised her as the girl from the party; he had checked her out plenty when she had been dancing, too.

'Yeah, well, her accent gets right on my tits,' snapped Paula, taking the joint from Ryan so that it bypassed Clea this time. She had also checked her out when she had been dancing, the horrible little snob.

'Look here,' said Clea. 'I don't appreciate your rudeness very much.' Paula picked up a plant and prepared to chuck it, dropping the joint on the floor in the process.

'Oy, oy, oy!' said Ryan, plucking the plant from her hands and retrieving the joint. 'What do you think you're playing at? Have some respect for my house.'

'You're fucking asking for it,' said Paula, pointing at Clea, her blue eyes icy.

The Frog Theory

Clea opened her mouth to reply.

'Don't you know when to leave it?' interrupted Kim, not wishing to see Clea plastered around the walls.

'I just don't understand why she's got such a problem with me,' said Clea.

'You're a snob,' said Paula. 'Never done a hard day's work in your life!'

'You don't know that,' said Clea. 'What a ridiculous thing to say.'

'I know enough. Coming 'round 'ere, leaving your coat on – 'fraid you might catch summink?'

'A bigoted attitude, maybe,' said Clea, getting up to leave. Walking around in the cold was preferable to this. Paula blocked her way.

'Who do you think you are?' Paula said, pushing her back into the room.

Before Kim or Ryan had a chance to intervene Clea swiped her leg around Paula's legs and pushed her shoulders. Thwack. Paula was on the floor and Clea soon had her in a body lock.

'You're fucking dead,' choked Paula

'Looks like it,' said Clea. 'I can get this grief at home, I don't need it from you.' With that, she released her hold and Paula sprang to her feet, breathing heavily, jumping from foot to foot like a fiery little bull.

For a moment, Clea's eyes met Kim's and she detected a spark of amusement. She resisted the urge to smile and left, taking the lift.

Kim went after her using the stairs and easily made it to the bottom first, leaning against the wall to wait.

'Smells of piss, doesn't it?' Kim said, smiling, when the doors opened on the ground floor to reveal Clea, holding her nose. 'That's why we use the stairs.'

Clea ignored him and began to walk fast – out of the building, off the estate. 'Wait,' said Kim, hurrying to keep up. He kept pace with her, thinking that she would probably speak eventually. 'Er...you walked past your street,' he said as she carried on down Hurlingham Road towards the bridge. She still hadn't said a word. 'Clea, come on, aren't you taking the silence thing just a little bit too far?'

At last, a reaction.

'A little bit too far?' she said. 'One of your mates tried to beat me up! That's what I call taking things a little bit too far.'

'Agreed,' said Kim. 'And I'm sorry about that, I really am.'

'It's what you think as well, though, isn't it? Because I've got a posh accent I have a nice little life with a...with a...' she stammered, thinking of Sarah. 'A loft full of pearls and a trust fund,' she finished.

'No,' said Kim defensively, before contradicting himself to say, 'Well, yes...I did think some of those things, you're right, though I don't know about the pearls...and I'm sorry because I've got to kind of like you.'

'Oh!' said Clea, thrown by his unexpected honesty.

They walked through the tunnel under Putney Bridge, up the steps next to Bishops Park, and stopped to look at the view.

It was like twilight, thought Clea, looking at the sparkling river with its promenade sweeping alongside it. Old fashioned street lamps threw small circles of warm dim light between evenly spaced wooden benches and after all the walking it didn't feel in the slightest bit cold. The moon had lit the tips of the trees with magnificent panache and she could do nothing but stare.

'Do you want to go in?' Kim asked, watching her rapt expression.

They sat on a bench next to the river and somehow Clea found herself telling Kim everything. Her argument with Sarah, who had been her only friend. How Hugo made her feel constantly watched, and trapped; that she had left the house wearing nothing but her underwear under her coat because he would have lost his temper if he'd answered the door and found a guy standing there. How *bored* she was being grounded and cooped up in her bedroom the whole time.

The Frog Theory

She stared out across the water.

'...And the joke is I can't seem to leave,' she finished. 'You'd think I'd be dying to get out of the place yet I stay and I don't fight or protect myself.' She hung her head in shame. 'I don't understand how I can fling someone like Paula to the floor yet when it comes to him...' she trailed off as she so often did.

'It's clear to me,' said Kim.

'It is?' she said, looking at him.

'Hugo's got the hots for you and what's he going to tell himself? That he fancies a kid he's known since birth and is meant to be a father figure to, over his own wife? That he's a sad old pervert? Or that you're a terrible kid who needs disciplining for your own good and he's doing you a favour by smacking you about?' He started rolling a joint. 'Everyone's their own best spin doctor, Clea.'

She let his words sink in. Hugo fancied her. It made sense of all the times she'd felt the need to cover herself, the horrible feeling he was trying to catch her naked when he burst into her room unexpectedly. The inappropriate things he said. But he was so much older, husband to her mother and the nearest thing to a father she had, she didn't want to believe it.

'So why don't I get out?' she asked at last.

'The frog theory,' Kim answered decisively. She hadn't heard of the frog theory and asked him to explain.

'You must know that old thing. You put a frog in boiling water – it jumps out and lives, but if you put it in cold water and heat it up slowly...stays in and dies.' He licked the edge of the Rizla and stuck it along the cone. 'Wonder what sick fuck found that out?' he said as an afterthought.

From kid to teenager, Clea had grown up in that house with the violence slowly escalating. Maybe it was already too late and she would never be strong enough to get out?

'Oy!' said Kim, nudging her away from her thoughts. 'Don't miss a great night because of that arsehole, Clea.' He handed her the joint.

It was her turn to look at *him* properly for the first time. She felt like he was showing her how to get out of jail and her tummy flipped. Green eyes, yes. But also, tiny shards of platinum, lit somehow from within, orbiting his irises. *Planets!* She amused herself; she was migrating there with paralyzing intensity. She didn't realise it but the joint from earlier was kicking in. He looked out over the water once more, breaking eye contact, leaving her flailing. She had to stop banging on about herself, she had been the one to bring them to this depressing place. Frantic, she searched her mind for something light-hearted to say, somewhere else to take them – *a silly limerick.*

'A creature of charm is the gerbil, its diet's exclusively herbal. It grazes all day, on bunches of hay, passing gas with an elegant burble.' But not that, *noooo!* Why had she said it out loud? 'There's no profound moral behind it like there is with yours of course…' she trailed off, going seriously red and hiding behind her hair in possibly the biggest cringe of her life so far. The urge to giggle was almost irresistible, coming seemingly from nowhere.

'Maybe us smoking herb made you think of it?' said Kim, laughing. Not at the limerick but at the way she'd come out with it in her self-conscious way.

The chemistry bubbled, the metaphorical test tube brimmed. Kim kept Flow firmly in mind, his emotions in check – this wasn't so bad.

They talked.

A lot.

And time passed.

She was quick-witted and funny, interesting, too. The more they spoke, the less she stuttered and hid behind her hair. He connected with her mentally in a way that didn't generally happen, even with Flow. 'Listen to this,' he said eventually, handing her one half of his headphones, trying to forget that she was wearing nothing but her underwear beneath that coat.

Some sort of pumping dance music was playing, similar to the stuff she'd heard coming from one of the flats on the estate, and she loved it. 'Good, isn't it?' said Kim, closing his eyes.

The Frog Theory

They sat listening. The music and the gentle buzz of the joint had relaxed her and she moved closer to him, her shyness temporarily gone.

'Kim, will you kiss me?' she found herself asking softly. 'I've never been kissed before.'

It didn't cross her mind that his friendship with Flow would stop him. Flow was engaged to Jackie, after all, so when Kim jumped up like he'd been prodded with a hot poker, an action that pulled the headphone abruptly from her ear, she incorrectly assumed it was because he found the idea repulsive.

'You should go home. Hugo...all that,' he said. 'Didn't realise...look at the time.'

Being rejected by Kim hurt more than Hugo slapping her face.

He insisted on walking her home but she said next to nothing. After an uncomfortable goodbye, he made his way to the roof of the Glass Block, a favourite hangout of his and Flow's. It was a clear night and you could see the whole of London twinkling below. He thought perhaps it would help him shake the horrible feeling that something was wrong. Instead, he remembered that he had failed to get Clea's number.

The main thing was that he hadn't kissed her, though, despite wanting to very much. He wasn't putting his best friendship on the line for anybody.

He texted Flow two question marks which simply told him, in their language – *I'm on the roof of the Glass Block if you want to come.*

Jackie was sleeping after sex but Flow was wide awake. The engagement celebration had gone by in a blur whilst two questions circled his mind – why was Ryan phoning his girlfriend; *correction-* fiancée? And why was he, himself, finding another girl attractive?

* * *

Checking Jackie's phone might answer one of those questions but personal integrity stopped him. Personal integrity, who was he kidding? He had failed to guess her password.

One more try, he decided, then he would give up. He reached stealthily over the sleeping Jackie, his own phone vibrating just as he was about to grab hers. Bzzzzzzzz. It gave him a guilty start.

? ?

The roof of the Glass Block was exactly what he needed right now. He pulled his clothes on, making as little noise as possible, and grabbed his backpack containing his spray paints. The opportunity to practise his art often arose on these spontaneous excursions.

'You're not going out?' said Jackie, stirring. 'It's gone midnight.'

He was – and that was that.

He climbed onto the roof of the glass block via the lift shaft, the only way to get to it without a key, and saw Kim with a beer in his hand, looking at the stars.

'So?' Flow asked. 'Did you call for her?'

'Uh huh,' said Kim.

One look at Flow's face made him feel relieved that he hadn't messed up. He subconsciously touched the scar on the side of his head, it was strangely addictive.

Flow sat next to him, cracked open a beer.

'Fuck that's good,' he said, after a lot of glugging.

Kim gave Flow a synopsis of the evening with Clea, leaving out the part about the kiss that wasn't a kiss. Flow didn't even mention the phone number, he just launched into a confession of all his doubts and fears concerning his relationship with Jackie, so Kim didn't bring it up either, he simply listened.

It did briefly cross his mind that if Jackie had something going on with Ryan it would explain why she had made the

The Frog Theory

effort to go all the way to the New Forest, but he quickly dismissed it as impossible. Ryan simply wouldn't do that.

They checked their crop of grass, congratulating themselves on the contraption they had built which ran neatly off the same electrics as the communal hallways and lifts, then took a shortcut up Clea's road, their favoured route to the all-night kebab shop.

Kim stopped abruptly to eye up a pristine Porsche.

'That belongs to Clea's stepdad, doesn't it?' he commented. 'The dick who split her lip open?'

Flow had seen Hugo getting in and out of that distinctive car plenty of times when they'd worked near there – *Yes*.

Kim observed as Flow sprayed various colours, deep in his zone, in awe as the caricature of Hugo quickly emerged. It was an absolute gift, he never tired of watching him and laughed all the way to the kebab shop thinking of the completed article.

A police car sidled by and two coppers peered at them suspiciously. Without thinking, Flow spat his gum hard and it hit one of the windows.

'Agup,' said Kim.

'Dagown,' said Flow. With that they ran in opposite directions like the wind. 'Dagoragia!' yelled Flow over his shoulder.

'Bragoomhagouse,' shouted Kim over his. Adrenalin pumped through him as he ran and the power of his strides made him feel like he was running to a satisfying rhythm that was speeding up and fuelling him.

They had been speaking in their childhood secret language – back slang. (Also known as Pig Latin.) You put an 'ag' before vowels and it sounded like gobbledygook, but to them it made perfect sense. Useful in all sorts of situations. Translated : Ag**up** – up. **D**ag**own** – down. **Brag**oomh**agouse** – Broomhouse, **D**agor**agia** – Doria.

Kim hid up on the roofs in Broomhouse Lane and Flow hid down on the ground in Doria Road. The speed with which they did it meant that the police hadn't even worked out which one to follow first – they were nowhere to be seen by the time they tried. They weren't going to get helicopters out or spend very long on such a small incident. After a couple of minutes, they heard the siren fire up and disappear into the distance, they had been called to something more important.

Flow sprinted to the kebab shop, knowing that Kim would need pacifying.

'Idiot,' said Kim scornfully, immediately softening when Flow handed him the much- needed food.

'Gotta keep fit,' Flow said, cramming chips into his mouth, not in the least bit fazed by the trouble he'd just caused.

Mr Whippy

'Hugo – it looks like you,' said his wife in amazement, referring to the caricature on the driver's side window of her husband's car. It depicted a man in a Mr Whippy cap, licking the top off an ice cream, with a ludicrously long tongue.

'Don't be so bloody ridiculous,' puffed Hugo, hyperventilating. 'How could it possibly look like me?'

Somehow his once beautiful car had been turned into an ice cream van overnight and he was still pinching himself, convinced he was dreaming and would wake up any minute.

The police were filling in a report and asking him lots of questions, swiftly discovering that Hugo was not the most personable of men. They surveyed the images of iconic ice creams and lollies with perplexed expressions. They had never come across a crime of this sort before.

'Are you sure nobody's got a vendetta against you, Mr Templar?'

'Or a cornetta?' quipped the other policeman, pleased with his joke. It didn't improve Hugo's mood.

From her vantage point at an upstairs window, it was only Clea who noticed Kim and Flow sitting at a safe distance on one of the roofs opposite, casually witnessing the fracas unfolding below.

Although she laughed, she ached with pain and embarrassment that Kim had refused to kiss her and she never wanted to see him again. How could she have thought that someone like him would have wanted to kiss someone like her?

Nonetheless, she felt deeply touched that they would make Hugo's car into an ice cream van for her and the heartbeat of their world hammered in hers, filling the spaces with evocative thuds.

Maybe the world heard it hammering too.

The car had to be towed to the local body shop for the damage to be photographed and assessed. One of the mechanics thought it was funny to order a 99 ice cream from Hugo and soon found that this was no laughing matter. It was going to take them all day to fill out forms, rent a car to tide them over and to get an official report from the police station for the insurance company.

So Clea was by herself in the house when a stranger came to the door. He explained that he represented a firm of solicitors handling an inheritance in connection with her biological father.

She asked whether that meant her father was dead but he was not at liberty to say. Her next question was whether she needed to bring her mother. She was eighteen and legally an adult, so that was up to her. There was either an opening now, or not for another week. She opted for now.

The solicitor

The solicitor asked Clea to sit down. Eyes of warm brown and a demeanour that was professional swept over her. He had been appointed executor of the will with instructions to present a letter to the sole beneficiary – *her*, in the event of his client's death.

As soon as she heard the soft click of the office door closing she tore the envelope open and unsheathed the handwritten letter. Clea knew nothing about her father, only that he had left when she was very young.

Dear Clea,

What do you say to a daughter you've never met? For a start, if you're reading this, I'm dead. Not the greatest way to introduce myself, I admit, and

I apologise. However, best to get the bad news over first, so moving swiftly on.

I met your mother when I was a young man of twenty-two and was very taken with her fragile beauty. She was a lady of few words, which I took to signify mystery, depth and intrigue. I was wrong. It turned out that she was dull, selfish and shallow.

I had already decided to leave her when I discovered she was pregnant with you. I could have kept in touch and all that, but commitment is not my strong point and I have always believed in pursuing one's own pleasures, rather than trying to please every other bugger.

I have enjoyed many affairs and have travelled extensively. Unfortunately, I have been stupid enough to keep trying my hand at marriage and now face divorce yet again, it has driven me to drink and to feel frightfully sorry for myself.

I surmised that you might come and find me when you were old enough, if you had any gumption, or a romantic notion that meeting me would somehow enrich your life, a bridge I would have crossed if necessary.

A discussion with the latest divorce lawyer, who was almost as dull as your mother, prompted me to leave you everything in my will in the unlikely event of an untimely death, so that the bloody government didn't snaffle it. The bloody wife will have had at least half, of course.

Enjoy,
Dad.

Clea didn't wait long before calling the solicitor back to the room; it was too much to take in. He asked whether he could read the letter and when he was through she was pretty sure she heard him mutter 'bloody idiot' under his breath.

He shook his head sadly.

'Well,' he said, laying the offensive item on the desk. 'He clearly didn't expect this to come to fruition and he was certainly under the influence of alcohol and whatever else whilst writing, but still…' He left the sentence hanging sympathetically in the air.

People so often hurt their young irrevocably. Not on purpose, he generously chose to think. He was a family man with two daughters and a son, whom he loved very much. He had sacrificed his pursuit of acting in favour of supporting them, in fact, by becoming a solicitor – thus generating regular income and a guarantee of work.

Life had hurled an injured little bird at his feet, he thought, rather theatrically – *how best to splint her wings?* He decided to drop his professional demeanour and to give this young lady his attention.

He left the formality of his desk and took her hands in his own. It didn't give Clea the creeps the way it would have if Hugo touched her; instead, it made his compassion tangible as he explained how her father had been killed in a pile up on a motorway in Spain. She felt for the first time in her life that her feelings were precious to somebody.

Her father had always meant to rewrite the letter, he had dashed it off during one of his visits to England, drunk and in a hurry, mid-divorce, but he would never be able to rewrite it now.

Clea asked what he had been like and the solicitor was able to tell her bits and pieces that helped her conjure some sort of picture. He described him as a lively entrepreneur with a zest for life and told her a couple of anecdotes. He left out (for now) functioning alcoholic, hopelessly addicted to women, just divorced for the third time.

After the solicitor's PA had delivered two hot chocolates, he unlocked the drawer of a filing cabinet and produced a bag of mini marshmallows. Clea felt her eyebrows rise slightly in surprise. *Shhhhh!* he indicated, incongruously childish.

The Frog Theory

He opened the packet and dropped a few into the top of her drink and then a few into his own.

'You have to wait until...' He stared expectantly into his mug. She found herself peering into her own. He prodded tentatively with a teaspoon then apparently satisfied that the moment was right, hoiked a few into his mouth and sucked indulgently. Clea copied.

Insanely sweet. Silky, spongey, something? *Oh dear!* She wanted to laugh and the solicitor enjoyed seeing the transformation in her expression, exactly the shift in tempo he had been hoping for, something to break the metaphorical ice.

'You've been left a life-changing amount of money, perhaps we could discuss what are you going to do next?' he asked kindly.

'What are you *meant* to do when someone is hitting you at home?' she blurted, cross with herself immediately. 'I'm not asking for myself,' she lied pathetically. 'It's for my friend at school...I thought while I was here and we were talking...' She dropped her gaze as he clearly wasn't fooled for a second. 'I mean...I don't think it's that bad...I think he just slaps her now and again and...calls her some rude names but...' she trailed off.

'Try taking a breath before you speak, that way you will not blurt whatever is on your mind.' She felt relieved that he had been so gracious. 'You asked what to do when someone is hitting you at home...well, there is such a thing as a restraining order so that the person can no longer go near you without the threat of jail but that means said person has to be tried and convicted in a court of law first...which takes time...then there is something called an injunction that can be applied for at a police station and...'

'Stop,' said Clea. 'Please.'

These were the sorts of discussions that had prevented her from saying anything at school for so long. Any of those actions would result in unpredictable ramifications – social services, *court*, taken to a foster home, labelled 'abused' – she didn't want any of it and now she was eighteen, she didn't *have* to have any of it.

The money seemed cold and meaningless – she would swap it a thousand times over for a loving family. 'Sorry...I just needed time to think.' She kept her hand in his; it was surprisingly reassuring and comforting. 'If I needed money today, could I get some?'

'How much are you asking for?'

She had no idea how much a hotel might cost. 'A thousand pounds, maybe?'

'I could give you a bridging loan,' said the solicitor. He had his own family to support and this was possibly beyond the call of duty – but still.

'This is going to sound crazy but...I have to leave while the water is boiling, they won't be back for ages today, they're sorting out Hugo's stupid Porsche.'

The solicitor raised an eyebrow.

'I'll explain next week when I come back...this is something I've got to do now, I promise I won't let you down.'

Smash the mask

Clea went home and thought about her belongings. What was she going to need for her new life? Her passport. Her birth certificate. That was all she legally needed in order to be a citizen of the United Kingdom and all she actually wanted to take.

Clea Scott-Davis, she read thoughtfully. Her mother had never legally changed her name to Hugo's – *good*.

She began to stack all her things in the garden. She went through her poems, photographs and various belongings and soon had quite a pile.

Into the haphazard heap, she stuck twigs and fire-lighters from the barbeque, scrunched up pieces of paper; other items that would catch easily. She opened a box of matches. W*oo-i-ck sssshush*, struck the first. The second. A third. Offering the flame

The Frog Theory

here and there soon made a bonfire. Uniform, clothes, shoes, boots, toothbrush, the stupid coat she had worn the night she had gone out naked.

She worried for a moment that the fence was going to catch as glowing got to crackling and smoke began to billow but most significantly, she worried about how she was going to feel about this in a few weeks, months or even years. There was no way of knowing, only faith that there must be something better than this.

She felt an almighty wrench as the reality of it all hit her heart. She was leaving home. She was leaving *them*, her only family – it was her first major life decision, the first time she had truly taken control.

The moments of violence played vividly in her mind, the shoe-hitting incident taking centre stage. She reflected upon her mother's apathy to Hugo's behaviour throughout – her – life.

She thought once again that she would give back the money she had inherited a thousand times and more in exchange for a loving family, it's all that kept taunting her but the money was her golden ticket out, and she must seize it.

The heat of the blaze threw an oily, transparent shimmer between herself and her things. Her soul had been dull – saturated with self-doubt and fear for so long, it was sick.

Rage coursed through her, fuelled by the knowledge that she was never coming back. She ran into the house. She had heard that in some cultures, slamming the door ten times, when you moved into somewhere new, got rid of demons.

Smash, smash, smash went the door, the force of her fury expunged. Maybe it would work the other way around and help to jettison the bad memories. By the time she had got to the tenth, the door hung off its hinges and she left very calmly, her belongings nothing but a smouldering pile of ashes in the garden.

She didn't look back; she looked forward to the main road at the end of the street and at the black taxis that regularly went down it, displaying their alluring yellow lights on top of their roofs like cheery beacons of hope. This time she was going to stop one and it was going to take her to a new life.

Smart shoes

The principal had just settled down at her desk to catch up on some paperwork when a young man burst into her office without knocking.

'Hello,' she said pleasantly.

'I want to come to your college.' Kim looked at her bashfully, taking in her smart shirt and jacket. He was taken aback by how attractive she was and felt very young and stupid all of a sudden.

'Why do you want to come to my college?' she asked, mildly flattered by the way he looked at her, but used to it.

Kim looked at the floor.

'If you're not prepared to sell yourself there are plenty of others who are,' the principal snapped impatiently.

'Fuck!' said Kim.

'That's a start,' said the principal.

'Sorry,' he mumbled. 'I think I should stop wasting your time.' The principal went back to her paperwork dismissively.

Kim was used to teachers and probation officers making an effort, trying to understand him, gently coaxing; this was new. 'What kind of fucking teacher are you? You don't know anything,' he accused. It had taken a lot for him to come here and *try* for once in his life. 'Sitting behind there in your smart suit with your smart nails and your smart hair and, and...' he searched for something else to say.

'My smart shoes?' she suggested with a raised eyebrow.

Kim shifted awkwardly.

'I couldn't see your shoes.'

From the waist down, she was concealed by a large, low-skirted desk. Strewn across it were some personal letters to an address in Chelsea. He had a photographic memory and knew now the details would remain. 'I'm sure they're smart, though,' he added politely as an afterthought, wishing to appear respectful after a less than perfect beginning.

'Sit down and tell me your name,' said the principal.

He did as he was told.

Kim Carter. She tapped it into her computer, a computer with a difference. It had a link-up with the police and social services. It had been just one of many things she'd relentlessly slashed through red tape for. She could find out anything about anybody who was or had been in trouble – that way she could see the full picture straight away and be more effective at helping.

She pulled Kim's files. Ah, yes, it immediately flagged up a strong recommendation from his probation officer that he attend her college. She scanned his history. Poor attendance at school and lots of trouble with the police for petty crimes, some more serious, including stealing a red London bus with a youth called Frank Young.

So, he had a sense of humour.

'Are you still friends with Frank?' she asked.

Kim had to think for a moment before he realised she was talking about Flow – Frank was his real name. He explained that Flow was his best mate.

How had she known that?

'I know everything,' said the principal, as if she had read his mind.

There was nothing violent in Kim's history, she was pleased to see. He was extremely bright, too, had passed various exams despite his poor attendance.

Social services had been on and off the scene throughout his childhood because of a mother who was a prostitute but he had never actually been taken into care. His father was unknown.

She looked at him more carefully, giving him her full attention for a moment. Her focus made Kim want to buckle at the knees.

The Frog Theory

'My PA will give you all the forms you need and direct you to the careers' officer,' she said, still observing him closely. 'And...' she lost track, something about him pierced her initial layer – not a pleasant sensation.

'Yes?'

'Welcome to this college.'

'Thank you...very much,' said Kim respectfully, taking his leave.

Must try harder

Jackie's secret phone calls from Ryan had been eating Flow and he had tackled her on the subject.

Good thing, too, because he had got it all wrong. Ryan and Jackie had been planning a secret engagement present for him, which hadn't arrived yet. What present Ryan could be helping Jackie with was a mystery to Flow but she said that was the whole point of a surprise.

While she had been so generous and thoughtful, he had been doubting her and fantasising about another woman. Jackie was not talking to him and he had suffered their worst argument yet.

There had been tears on her part, accusations of trust issues, reminders of everything she had done for him since they had been together – amid a lot of high-pitched yelling, all of which had left him feeling like a guilty monster.

He was going to get a regular job, start making something of his life as Jackie had suggested. She had said that he would never get anywhere with his art, that it was childish and he should be thinking about their future together, earning an honest living.

That was why he was at the barber's having his hair cut, looking at the job adverts. He wanted to go to Jackie physically changed as well as mentally changed to show that he was sorry. He resolved to treat her better and to give things his best shot, she deserved that.

* * *

It was a different Flow who stood on Jackie's doorstep. Instead of the shoulder length curls he now sported a crop. He looked manlier, somehow, and wiser. She liked what she saw but also felt uneasy. Flow was finding a sense of himself and she was scared he would pull away from her and that other women were going to start finding him attractive.

Coming up with a surprise engagement present that she could say involved Ryan had given her a massive headache but she had done it. She had bought him a car on hire purchase. (Ryan knew a lot about cars.) Her job at Boots didn't pay much but it was regular and she had never been overdrawn at the bank, so securing finance had been relatively easy.

Ryan had been useless; he wasn't the least bit interested in helping her get out of the predicament. She had knocked their little affair on the head, fooling herself that he was upset.

The initial buzz of an indiscretion gave her ego a satisfying shot and was as addictive as any other drug. She wasn't going to be one of those women who trusted their men blindly only to be walked over, she was going to be ahead of the game.

Flow was different from what she saw as the 'big catches', the Ryans and Kims of this world, who took a lot more to pin down. He was still pretty immature and doted on her, she wasn't going to let that go in a hurry.

The Ritz

The Ritz Hotel had immediately popped into Clea's mind when the taxi driver had asked where she was going, so she had said it. And now here she was, sitting on the edge of a large bed in a fancy room, sipping a cup of mint tea. She carefully constructed a text to the solicitor, on the phone he had lent her. He said she should call him by his first name, Charlie. That made it more personal and much easier.

> Have booked into the Ritz for the night as it was the only hotel I could think of in a hurry. Is very nice.
> See you tomorrow as planned. C

The Frog Theory

The only hotel she could think about in a hurry, I should Coco, what had he been thinking? But steady, Charlie, he told himself. He must believe in her.

> Good for you! Enjoy and I will
> see you tomorrow. Ch

They were to meet in the British Library, of which he was a member, so that Clea did not have to return to his office in Fulham and run the risk of bumping into her mother, or Hugo.

He explained that he had been appointed sole executor of her father's estate and after what was called 'the granting of probate', which he had already applied for, he would be able to distribute the funds.

'Even if I was a magician I couldn't have arranged things better for you, Clea...your father had just finalised a divorce and had put his entire share of the proceeds into an English bank account, ready to reinvest in property and other funds in Britain, where he had decided to relocate once more. Basically, after expenses and inheritance taxes you will have (give or take) enough cash sitting in a bank for you to be financially independent.'

She tried to look grateful but was still horribly overwhelmed by the entire thing. She gazed at the impressive surroundings and vaulted ceilings. Books upon books could be viewed through round windows from their position in the members' room, incomprehensible amounts of information swirled around them.

She had been looking up stories of amazing women, whilst at the Ritz, to give her inspiration. The story that had touched her the most was the life of a polish lady called Irena Sendlerowa, who had helped Jewish families save their children from the Nazis. She had trained a dog to bark when she told it to, so that when the smaller children cried, it would distract the Nazi guards and cover up the noise. She hid children in sacks, in bags full of clothes, in boxes. In three months, she saved 2,500 children. Clea felt the tears spring to her eyes, thinking of it.

'Clea, are you even listening to me?'

'Yes, sorry; you were saying that after the granting of probate you thought I would be able to get the money in about three months…that I basically had a pile of cash.'

'So, I'm suggesting you stay in the annex at my house in South Kensington while you wait for the money and decide what to do…my mother uses it when she comes to London sometimes…but it has its own door…its own key, you would have your privacy.' And I can't afford the bloody Ritz every night, he thought to himself.

There were various bills to be paid, of course – taxes upfront would be due and his own account would need settling, but he had already decided he would take care of those things without burdening Clea further. There was also the question of her father's belongings, making their way by sea-freight from Australia, towards England, as they spoke. Another detail he would leave out for now.

Clea turned her mind to Bethany Hamilton-Dirks, a professional surfer who had survived a shark attack in which her left arm had been bitten off. Even after that, the courageous girl had not only dared to get back in the water but had returned to compete at surfing, victorious. Clea tried to imagine life with one arm. She put one of her own behind her back for a moment, and sat on her hand, her imagination flying. 'Are you quite alright, Clea?' Charlie asked, looking perplexed.

'I was trying to imagine what it would be like to have one arm!' blurted Clea, going red and hiding behind her hair.

'I'm sorry, I'll slow down. It's a lot to take in…let's change the subject for a while.'

Clea felt the need to elaborate on the reason for her strange behaviour and told Charlie about her findings, the way she felt so inadequate next to these extraordinary women.

Charlie listened patiently, although he had many matters to attend to that day.

The Frog Theory

'Hmm, there's one thing both those women had of which you have been sorely short-changed, Clea.'

She flicked her hair slightly to the side so that she could meet his gaze, transfixed by whatever he was going to say next. 'Love, my dear girl, I believe that both those incredible women knew what it was to be unconditionally loved.'

She looked at him blankly. 'It's not to be underestimated. Stand up.' She did as she was told. He wrapped her in an almighty bear hug and she felt herself relax as she succumbed to an energy greater than hers. All the tension started to leave her body, she literally began to feel uplifted. 'People need people, Clea,' he explained, returning to his chair. 'Now, once you've checked out of the Ritz, make your way to this address.' He pushed a piece of paper across to her and also a set of keys. He got up, an indication that it was time to leave. She followed his cue and they walked to the lift together. 'I'll be home at about seven and I'll come to check how you've settled in,' he said, before striding off towards the Tube.

The annex was a dear little place. She supposed it was what people would describe as a bedsit – a good-sized, single room, containing a double bed, a little sofa and a kitchen along one wall. In one corner sat an old-fashioned café style table for two, and off to the side there was a quaint bathroom, with a good-sized bath.

Her night at the Ritz had cost nearly half the cash Charlie had given her and she had no clothes or food, so after her recce she set off to get some basic necessities.

Charlie checked in around seven, as promised, and asked her to come to the main house for dinner, to meet his family. She explained that she had to get stronger first, that she wasn't ready, not yet. She begged him – personal space. That was all she craved.

He respected her wishes but reappeared a few minutes later with a small dog in his arms.

'Meet Flash,' he said. 'Everybody needs somebody, Clea.'

He handed her the enthusiastic, panting ball of fluff, leaving her speechless.

She relished her time in the annex, enjoying the freedom of not being watched, apart from by Flash, who had become a regular house-guest.

She found herself growing and unfurling in her new surroundings. The peaceful atmosphere nurtured her newly developing confidence, and the realisation that she enjoyed her own company.

She soon discovered that Charlie was an extremely busy man. He worked long hours but she could always text him if she needed to and she enjoyed her privacy, so she did not feel in any way deserted. He had fixed her up with enough money to have total independence whilst she waited for her father's estate to be settled so she didn't have to bother him when she wanted food.

It was enough to pay for clothes, a computer, even a car, if she had so wished. She wasn't sure of the mechanics of it all but Charlie had told her not to worry and to focus on planning her life, and that is what she was doing. Humbled by his kindness, she wanted to please him.

She got a laptop to help her research and plan. Her heart was in acting and dancing, it was her natural talent which she had expressed so far mostly through gymnastics, inhibited as she was in the past by Hugo. Once 'on stage' she could become something else and lost all her inhibitions.

She had been in contact with Cours Florent, in Paris, and had decided to take their spring session – acting in English, open to students over the age of seventeen with no previous experience required. It was a first step toward something that she loved.

Whenever she left the annex, she imagined Hugo was going to jump out from somewhere. A stint abroad would free her from that fear while she built a foundation for her life.

French has been one of the subjects that were compulsory at school, and after purchasing her laptop, she had bought an online course, so that she could become as fluent as possible before relocating. Keeping busy with all these things stopped her mind from going to dark places.

She had both her arms and she was not trying to hoodwink Nazis with the lives of 2,500 children in her hands. These comparisons helped to spur her on.

'*Je vous en prie.*' *You're welcome* – she answered her conversational French program, as she pottered around the place.

Message in a bottle

When Flow sheepishly admitted to Kim that he had decided to stay with Jackie after all, Kim had kicked himself for not getting Clea's number. He wanted to see her again, to say yes to that kiss. He casually wandered past her house a few times, hoping to bump into her.

A week had gone by then two, but still no luck. He knew the trouble it would cause if he rang the bell and her stepfather answered, so instead he wrote a note, which he rolled up and slid into a beer bottle. He then climbed her house in the middle of the night and left it on her bedroom windowsill, partially hidden by the ivy. He peered into her bedroom while he was at it but she was not there.

He knew she liked to lean out of the window for the odd cigarette late at night and he felt sure she would find it, but the weeks had gone by and still he had seen and heard nothing.

He hoped that she was okay, but he hardly knew her, and didn't want to come over like a stalker. Maybe when the buzz had worn off, after that night at the park, she had realised she preferred Flow over him. Whatever the reason, she didn't contact him, so he shoved her from his mind and resolved to forget her.

It was probably for the best, he got the feeling that it might have been awkward with Flow, anyway and he had other things to think about. Kim had come to terms with the inevitable responsibility approaching and had got Leigh to fill in lots of papers with him to secure a council flat. She looked very beautiful pregnant, glowing and fresh, but the mental spark wasn't there and he wasn't going to get trapped into 'being a couple' no matter what pressure she applied – which was plenty. Still, he was going to make sure he provided for his child.

Bad vibrations

The principal lay back on her bed and reached into the top drawer of her bedside table where her vibrator was kept. Without it, she would be a frigid old wreck. It was a regular necessity that she abstained from when the children were at home, another reason to be relieved when they went back to school.

Since Mike, she had been unable to connect emotionally or physically with herself, let alone another person. She was locked in an emotional stalemate; the vibrator was purely functional, with no spontaneity or genuine pleasure about it.

Usually she wouldn't think about anything controversial, she would simply let things take their course as quickly as possible and put it away again but lately, there had been a certain student breaking into her thoughts.

It bothered her deeply; she had never had a crush on a student, ever. It broke her rhythm and made her stop, until she had managed to get Kim Carter out of her head.

She saw the way he looked at her whenever they met in college. It was like he could see something that wasn't purely skin deep. A chemistry existed between them that was tangible and out of control, and as is often the way with these things, it was as if they were in an invisible sphere, seemingly drawn together; for whenever she walked down a corridor or left her office, their paths seemed destined to cross.

It was unsettling; one guilty secret was more than enough.

* * *

The Frog Theory

Dear Diary,

Clea's gone. I'm relieved, really, are you surprised? She left all her things in a smouldering heap in the garden.

Hugo pretended it was good riddance but I saw that muscle twitching in his cheek, indicating fury. I often wonder why he hates her so much.

I couldn't stand to watch her, feeling like a withered old fruit myself. I couldn't tell her my life was about unpredictable Catherine wheels, flinging incidents and nasty shocks, little disappointments, leaving their horrible burns.

I'm one of those people that it 'got' in a slow, patient, invisible way. Nothing dramatic like a fire or a plane crash. It's the little things that you don't notice at first, this bill, that wrinkle, the murder on the news. It all starts to build an invisible cage. What hope did I have to give her?

No, she's better off away from me, that's why I'm glad.

'So, Charlie, I've decided what I am going to do,' said Clea. 'I'm going to live in Paris for six months.'

'Okay,' said Charlie. 'Sounds good, tell me more.'

That was the great thing about Charlie, he was open-minded and supportive of her dreams, he treated her like an adult. She explained the research she had done into dance schools and academies, and the course she had chosen at Cours Florent.

Moneywise, Charlie had advised her to keep things simple. He suggested spending half of her inheritance on a property somewhere in London, and half on a varied pot of investments with the support of a financial advisor, who he could recommend.

The property would generate rent and the investments would generate dividends, creating enough in total to support her, whilst keeping her capital secure.

'So, are you ready to meet my family?'

Clea hesitated. She had given the subject a lot of thought and she still did not feel ready. It would be like having a box of chocolates put in front of her and finding that she couldn't help scoffing the lot, then being unable to move.

'I find it easier not to know what I have missed…I promise, Charlie…I will meet them when I come back. I will be ready then. Right now, I think if I met them I would never be able to leave the comfort of…well, you.'

He had no choice but to respect her wishes, odd as he found them.

Maybe baby

Flow honked the horn of his car three times and waited until he could see Jackie wave at him through the window of Boots in High street Kensington where she worked, before driving off to wait for her by the staff door.

He always tried to pick her up on a Saturday if he was anywhere near the area. The job hunting hadn't really gone that well so he had started cabbing. The money was good and it gave him the freedom to work extra hours whenever he wanted. Jackie and him had rented a small flat in Hammersmith together and were saving hard for the wedding.

Mindlessly he watched as the perfumery girls and shop people filed out, some chatting to friends, others meaningfully striding towards a car or familiar face.

It wasn't long before Jackie appeared, clicking her way towards him on high heels. He admired her compact figure and the air of purpose in her sexy walk and felt a stab of guilt that, despite his best intentions, he managed to disappoint her so often. His face broke into a smile as he prepared to kiss her hello and ask her how her day was; maybe he could break their savings plan for once and take her somewhere special tonight?

She got into the car and slammed the door hard, folding her arms. Since Flow had got his hair chopped off and had bought some new clothes, girls were showing more of an interest in him and she believed he was more than aware of it, testing it out. She hated it, made her blood boil, and she was determined that Flow wasn't getting away with it.

'What's up with you?' said Flow.

'You know what,' snapped Jackie.

'Suit yourself, I'm not going to try and guess.'

'I saw you eying up that girl.'

Flow let out a sigh of exasperation. He was getting pretty sick of her accusations, which were nearly always unfounded. He had no idea what girl she was imagining.

He put the stereo on loud and they drove home without discussing it, but he knew it wouldn't stop the argument that was surely coming.

Kim had received the call to say that the baby was on the way and had been ringing Flow constantly but he wasn't picking up, so he had long given up the idea of a lift in his cab. Nevertheless, he wasn't going to go through this without him.

Answer your phone, you prick!

At last he got through and found that Flow was in the middle of yet another humdinger of a row with Jackie. He was getting seriously worried that Flow was going to lose himself in her twisted clutches. Talking of twisted clutches, this one was fucked, he thought to himself as he drove, struggling to get Ryan's van through the gears. It had seen better days, having been nicked, hotwired, found and returned more times that any of them could count. Ryan had never got around to having a new ignition put in and it could be started with a screwdriver, penknife, or similar implement, which was handy local knowledge if you happened to need a vehicle and you had the good fortune to see it parked somewhere.

Kim hadn't got around to taking his driving test yet but he could drive well enough. He indicated right off Fulham Palace Road and swung into Biscay Road, to find Flow running towards him at a fair pace, looking harassed. He stopped before knocking him down and Flow dived into the passenger seat.

'Drive,' he instructed. Kim sped off as best he could in the old tin can white van but Jackie stood in the road blocking their path. 'Reverse.' Flow revised.

The Frog Theory

Kim whacked the van clunkily into reverse and backed up as fast as he could before doing an impressive and dangerous, fluky spin, which left them facing the other way around, miraculously missing any parked cars in the narrow street because of a large gap reserved for a removal lorry.

'What the fuck?' said Flow, holing his heart and hyperventilating.

'Relax,' Kim chided as Jackie's image shrank in the side mirrors.

The spin hadn't been in the plan, it had been an override reflex action to get them out of trouble fast, and it had rattled him too, but he wasn't going to show it. 'Thought you'd given up?' he said as Flow ripped the plastic off a packet of fags and stuck one in his mouth.

'Emergency,' Flow said, riffling through his pockets for a lighter. Kim pushed the electric van lighter down as a backup plan. 'Fuck,' said Flow, coming up empty handed. 'Fucking fucking fuck!' he swore. 'No light.'

The van cigarette lighter popped up and Kim passed it across.

'Em.' Flow grunted, muffled by the cigarette pursed in his lips. He held the orange glow against it and puffed frantically until he was surrounded by swirls of smoke. 'Ahhhhhhhhhh!' He breathed out and Kim didn't interrupt while Flow collected himself. 'I'm guessing the baby's on the way,' he surmised, once he'd had sufficient puffs to become vocal.

'You guessed right,' said Kim. They were nearly at the hospital now.

Kim and Flow found Leigh propped up in a hospital bed eating a slice of toast. 'Where's the baby?' Kim asked, his adrenalin high, heart pumping.

'It came really quick,' said Leigh. 'They've taken it away for some tests…nothing serious,' she said with a little shake of her hair. 'Just weighing him and stuff.'

'Him?' said Kim. 'A boy?'

She put her toast on the side table and ran her hand through her bleached blonde mane a couple of times. 'Yeah! A boy... maybe you should come back tomorrow?'

The idea of putting fatherhood off for another day felt like a huge relief – yet he had revved himself into such a frenzy that he felt like his brain was literally glitching and he didn't know what to do or say next.

'Going for a slash,' announced Flow, leaving him standing awkwardly like a forlorn child. Flow might be rubbish at detecting lies in Jackie – he loved her and love *could* be blind, but when it came to other people, there was no beating him.

Leigh had been caught out somehow, he knew it, and an informal little chat with the ward sister, plus a sneak preview of the baby, revealed her predicament.

With a little smile he returned to the ward.

Kim was standing exactly where he had left him, except that he had thrust his hands deeply into his pockets as if he was trying to push himself through the floor.

'Were you constipated or something?' he accused with a hurt expression, having been deserted in his moment of need.

'Sorry, mate,' said Flow, not offended. Kim was always cranky when he was uncomfortable in a situation and he was keen to get him out of this one as quickly as possible.

'Leigh says we should come back tomorrow...says the baby...'

'Routine checks,' interrupted Leigh.

'Say no more,' said Flow decisively, steering Kim away. 'Manjana!' he called over his shoulder, noticing that Kim was too traumatised to say anything at all.

'Leigh's baby isn't yours, he's black,' Flow said as they strode out of the hospital together.

'You what?' said Kim, confused. They stopped in their tracks and Flow watched whilst a series of expressions crossed his friend's face, resting eventually in one of sustained delight.

The Frog Theory

'Come on, idiot-boy,' he said, once more taking control. 'We're going to the pub.' They set off at a fair pace – this day had been thirsty work for both of them.

There were two pubs that Kim and Flow visited most frequently – a small one down a little side road called The Cottage, or the Durrell Arms on the main drag of Fulham Road, which was larger, livelier, and had pool tables. Tonight, they started at The Cottage, sitting at a small table with their pints.

Kim felt indescribably relieved, like a character in one of those cheesy films whose life had seemed set to go a certain way before a twist of fate had given them another chance. He kept taking great big breaths as if he was about to say something meaningful, only to expel a contented sigh.

'Will you stop doing that?' said Flow.

'Doing what?' said Kim.

'The big sigh thing, it's really annoying.'

Kim shrugged, he was unaware that he was doing it.

They sipped their pints, contemplating the room for a while.

'You did it again!' said Flow.

'What?'

'The fucking sigh thing.'

'Sorry,' said Kim. 'I'm not doing it on purpose...anyway, you annoy me *most* of the time.'

'Thanks,' said Flow. 'Dick,' he added. 'Don't look now... blonde by the door, red shirt. *Now* you can look.'

'Nice,' said Kim. It wasn't long before she was joined by a friend, and they took surreptitious glances whist silently sipping their beers.

The one good thing about Flow's arguments with Jackie was that it temporarily released him from his shackles so that he could relax, check out other women and generally be a lot happier.

In his abandon, Flow did a funny, squeaky sounding sneeze, which resulted in beer coming out of his nose – a silly amusement that set them giggling like a couple of children. They sat there quivering conspiratorially with their backs to the rest of the pub.

'What are you two laughing about?' said a female voice. They looked around to see the girls they had been eyeing up.

'You don't want to know,' said Flow, gathering himself.

'How about you buy us a drink?' said her friend.

'Ohhhhh no, I don't think so,' said Flow. 'I've just had a row with my fiancée and he's just lost a kid.'

'Looks like it.'

'Vodka and Coke,' said the other one, cheekily.

'Haven't you heard of sexual equality?' said Kim. 'You should be buying *us* drinks.'

'Okay,' said the first girl. 'What's it to be?' Kim and Flow exchanged glances.

'Are you serious?'

The girl crossed her heart seductively.

'In that case...' said Kim.

Worried sick

Flow put his key quietly in the lock, fully expecting Jackie to be asleep, so he was surprised to find her sitting cross-legged on the sofa, fully dressed – make-up smeared down her face from crying.

He prepared himself for the onslaught, going to the small, open-plan kitchen, to get some distance from her. He put the kettle on and placed teabags in two mugs, then peeled off his top, which smelt of cigarettes and kebab – flinging it onto a chair in the sitting room. Jackie looked longingly at his smooth back. Flow's mother was black and his father white. His skin was the most beautiful colour and so smooth.

The silence was unbearable.

'Where have you been?' she asked quietly.

'Out with Kim,' he answered truthfully.

They had shared a couple of drinks with the girls, to return the round, before ditching them kindly and moving on for some

The Frog Theory

pool, then a smoke on the roof of the Glass Bock, finishing things off nicely at about three in the morning with a kebab.

'I love you,' she said, choked up. 'Why do we keep arguing?'

Flow leant against the kitchen unit, crossed his arms and looked at the floor as the kettle bubbled. He dwarfed the kitchen area with his six-foot-three frame.

'Well?' she said.

'You tell me,' said Flow, pressing the lid of the freestanding bin so that it flipped up with a satisfying whoosh.

He poured boiling water onto the teabags and left them for a minute before stirring one around and pressing it against the side of the mug so that it moulded itself into the bowl of the spoon and stayed stuck there when he lifted it out. Now he applied his right index finger to the tip of the spoon, gripped the handle firmly with the left, facing it away from him like a slingshot and catapulted the bag expertly into the bin – splat. He repeated the well-practised routine – a satisfying game which left arcs of tea in its wake. It worked best with round teabags.

Ordinarily it would drive Jackie crazy because she was always cleaning old tea off the floor and sides of the kitchen units, but now all she could think about was how much she would miss him *and* the arcs of tea if he wasn't around.

'I know you look at other women,' said Jackie.

'Looking isn't doing anything about it though, is it?' said Flow, pouring the milk and adding sugar – two for him, a Sweetex for Jackie. The teaspoon clinked around the mugs.

'No...' said Jackie. 'But it still pisses me off.'

'You look at other men.'

She wondered what he knew.

'No, I don't,' she said defensively. He crossed the room in little more than two strides and handed her the cup of tea with the Sweetex in.

'Anyway, I'm going to bed.' As he made his way through the flat he heard her following him with busy little steps and felt a sense of being worn down and worn out. 'Can we talk about whatever it is you need to talk about another time?' he asked pleadingly, thinking longingly of his motorbike magazine, comfortable bed and perfect cup of tea.

She slapped his face.

'How dare you,' she yelled. 'I've been sitting here worried sick, you hear me? *Worried sick.*' She crossed her arms, angry tears in her eyes. 'Look at you. Like a massive child. Without me you'd be nothing, you hear me? Nothing!'

'Everyone hears you, Jackie,' said Flow calmly, thinking of the neighbours. 'I can't take this anymore. What do you want from me? Everything I do is wrong.'

'I want you to grow up and appreciate what you've got. You'll never find anyone as good as me, *never*, you hear? Think about everything I've done for you. The car! You wouldn't even be cabbing without me, you'd have no money apart from what you made drug dealing – you'd probably be in jail by now with raggedy long hair,' she said, warming to her subject as she created an alternative Jackie-less Flow. 'Do you know how many men would kill to go out with me?'

'How many?' said Flow.

'Lots,' she said. 'That's how many. I get offers all the time but I don't even look and there's you eyeing up that girl. I SAW YOU!' she screamed. 'I give everything to you; my love, my life and *this...this* is what I get,' she said, sinking to the floor crying. 'And I put up with it...I put up with it because I love you and I see...I see the man you *could* be.' She sobbed.

Was he really such a monster? Was he really so bad? And did he *really* eye up some girl without realising it?

His background was so loving and easy that he expected to find those qualities in others, looked for them – whereas Kim was objective. He perceived human nature as it really was, as it presented itself. In a way, Kim's mother had got him ready for the world better than any other parent he knew.

Kim had independence and an ability to look after himself in every way. He had done his own washing since he was eight and knew how to cook basic stuff from an even younger age:

beans on toast, baked potatoes in the microwave, then he could cook whatever you wanted as he got older.

Flow had tried to cook dinner for Jackie one night and when he was still in the kitchen an hour after starting, Jackie had found him trying to mash uncooked potatoes. How could he know that you were meant to boil them first? She had laughed until she cried and he had pretended it didn't bother him – Flow the joker.

Maybe he did need to grow up, maybe she was right.

He felt so lonely and broken. Where was the smiling, sexy, fun girl he enjoyed being with so much? Where was *good* Jackie? What had he done to make her behave this way?

Though he wouldn't change his family for the world or the way his mother had done everything for him – cooking, cleaning, ironing, washing – he envied Kim his ability to be alone and to look after himself.

Flow was oblivious to the role he played in Kim's life. Flow *was* Kim's strength, Kim's family – the reason he was able to function so well.

'Come on,' said Jackie, holding out her hand. He pulled her to her feet. 'Let's not argue, let's start fresh.'

How many times had he heard that before?

She stroked his chest, and worked her way downwards.

Maybe this time it would work, thought Flow.

Leigh's pickle

'You've got yourself into a right old pickle, haven't you?' Leigh's nan would have said.

'Yeah, a hot fucking chilli pickle, Nan, the kind that burns your arse off on the way out.' Leigh said out loud to the room before resting her head back in her hands, half expecting her nan's ghost to appear and chastise her for swearing.

It was at times like these that she wished she had female friends to turn to, but she had ended up sleeping with most of their boyfriends, at some point, which was never a good way to bond with women.

Her mum had been sympathetic about the mistaken identity of Leigh's baby, similar things had happened to her. She had three children by different dads, life was too short to try and plan it; *what's meant to be will be* was her motto.

She had suggested telling Kim the baby was a genetic throwback but Leigh knew it wouldn't wash. *Try to borrow a baby of a similar age?* Yeah, right, how long could they keep up *that* pretence? 'Just long enough to get the flat, love.' Leigh's mum had advised. 'He's a man, he's not going to come over that often.'

Nice attitude, thought Leigh, who was not yet so jaded. She was many things – needy, sex/drug mad, inclined to buying too many shoes, even, but never a lying, manipulative person. She therefore decided to come clean and so far, the numerous attempts at an appropriate text message were not going well. She surveyed the latest:

Baby not yours. Sorry. ☺

No. Not right. What was she going to do?

Doorbell.

Followed by muffled conversation and a slam as her mum let someone in, then a man's voice and footsteps to her bedroom door.

Kim.

She looked at him guiltily.

'Speak of the devil, I was just trying to text you,' she said, running her hand through her hair a couple of times and getting up, brushing herself down nervously as if she were dusty.

'Oh yeah?' said Kim.

'Yeah,' said Leigh. 'Thing is...' she began. 'Thing is.' She pointed towards the Moses basket in the corner.

He looked in the basket. 'I'm so stupid,' she said, bursting into tears.

Kim felt very sorry for her, there was no bad in Leigh, she was just a bit of a needy nymphomaniac was all.

'Come here,' he said, taking her in his arms. 'It's going to be okay, you'll see.'

'It was such a shock,' she spluttered. 'I was so sure it was yours then I saw it and I remembered the time with that other bloke.'

Kim wiped her charcoal grey tears with his thumbs.

'Look what you're doing to your mascara...we were never an item, you were always free to go with other blokes.'

'I'm really sorry,' she said.

'I know you are but it's okay,' said Kim. 'I think we can help each other out.' Now she was listening.

Since believing he had a child on the way, Kim had been working on a *legitimate* business idea that could supersede the hydroponics – a kick-arse renovation company.

Mick was always busy and made a decent profit. All he did was turn up on time and produce a practical, functional result. Raising that product and service a level would open things up to a bigger market and the more Kim imagined it, the more he knew it was within his reach.

He had been looking at the mechanics of getting a council flat with Leigh and they could still do that, as planned but instead of Leigh moving in straight away, Kim could have it for a year and refurbish it to a standard that could be used as a showcase. He could photograph it and build a website to generate business, *then* pass it onto Leigh.

She was happy and relieved. A flat to look forward to was better than no flat ever. A flat all decked out was even better.

Kim left Leigh to feed the baby and began to walk to the park, the business idea starting to take a pleasant, more solid form. His mind now turned to a less pleasurable subject; *Ryan and Jackie*.

A look had passed between them recently and the obviously intimate nature of it had puzzled Kim. Flow had looked out for him like no other, surpassing himself with his most recent sleuthing – so although there was probably nothing in it – and digging further required bypassing the sacred rule that said you kept yourself to yourself regarding other people's romantic situations, he put his friendship with Ryan on the line and asked him straight. Was he having a thing with Jackie?

Ryan couldn't answer. It was true. Kim shook his head in disbelief and disgust. He had been their mate from the beginning, and he had thought there would be some explanation that would prove he had been out of line.

'Kim, she came onto me,' he began to defend himself. Kim put his hand up to stop him talking – he already felt like hitting him, thinking of how Flow had struggled in that relationship and of all the times Jackie had shouted at him for supposedly looking at other women. 'It's over now, anyway, we finished it.'

Smack.

Ryan was out for the count in one hit. Paula came running over and Kim walked off before Ryan came to, because he knew he would only knock him out again.

Wake-up call

This wasn't going to be easy and required ammunition: Cigarettes. Puff. Skins. Beer. Whisky chaser. Good music (check music player in pocket). Location – *the roof of the Glass Block, of course.*

'What's up?' said Flow, appearing at the top of the lift shaft looking worried. Kim got straight to the point.

'Jackie and Ryan…it was true.'

'What? When did you find out – how?' said Flow, ashen.

Kim told him about Jackie turning up in the Forest of Dean at the building job – how he didn't say at the time but thought fleetingly it was odd.

'…there was this look between them in the park and it made me think of it again…I still didn't believe *that* but I wanted to check what was up…so I asked him straight today – knocked him out,' finished Kim, cracking open the bottle of whisky, cutting to the chaser.

'All those times she accused *me*,' said Flow with quiet fury, 'and it was her fucking about, that twisted bitch. She told me

The Frog Theory

I was a monster…ripped me up…I've been thinking I was the one with some sort of problem.'

'You're the sanest person I know…I'd have been put into care a thousand times if it wasn't for you, Flow and I didn't look out for you properly when I should have…forest of Dean…I should have said what was on my mind.'

'Going around suspecting everyone…it's no way, Kim…in a million years I didn't think Ryan would do that…he was both our mates.'

Flow's phone buzzed.

Jackie.

Two missed calls and a text.

> Worried sick. U've been gone hrs. How cld u do this 2 me?
> We agreed, no disappearing.
> U better b in casualty unconscious 2 do this 2 me again.
> If I don't hear frm u in 20 min I'm calling your mum + checking hospitals.

Flow knew she wouldn't do any of those things. She would sit at home and wait for him like a vicious guard dog the way she always did. Get a taxi all the way from Hammersmith to Fulham to look for him? Pay money? He didn't think so – and she wouldn't dare call his mum in the middle of the night.

He threw the phone off the roof as hard and as far as he could and watched it shatter in the distance.

Kim's phone buzzed.

Jackie.

> Is Flow with you?

He threw his phone of the roof as hard and as far as he could, too – solidarity. They could get new phones, new numbers, then the harpie couldn't call them.

'Here's what we're going to do,' said Kim, clear minded, starting another play-list before sitting down again. 'We're going to go into another business together, get off the estate, go places, you and me.'

The night was clear and there wasn't a siren to be heard in London that night. 'I'm getting the flat still, with Leigh...but she's going to keep living with her mum 'til it's done up so you can move in there, with me...you keep cabbing, work all hours to buy the materials and we'll kit it out together.' He took a swig out of the whisky bottle and handed it over to Flow. 'Every place we do will have your art on a wall somewhere, it'll be our trademark, like a brand – a signature – maybe a big piece sometimes, a whole wall...small other times, just a little tag, or even a quirk like...I don't know, I'll think of something. People like brands and names, trust me on that, makes it something special.

'Hmmm,' said Flow, momentarily distracted from his troubles as he joined Kim in his visions. He was hooked.

They discussed the ins and outs into the small hours. Kim would study during the day and at night they would do the place up. They would photograph it and build a website as they went along. After that they would get a refurbishment job, maybe even more than one, they imagined, and be out of the flat before the authorities caught on – hand it over to Leigh as planned.

Flow and Jackie had already saved a decent amount for the wedding and Flow would take his half out that night, before Jackie got wise. Even with what she'd done he didn't want to take more than his fair share – that was Flow. He would put the money into their new venture to start them off; what had happened with Ryan had not shaken the bond between himself and Kim, if anything, it had made them appreciate what they had even more.

'Fifty-fifty,' agreed Flow, that is how they would split everything as always, down the middle – half each. They shook on it, complete trust between them, no need for anything else. Even when the time came that they were earning millions – and that time was going to come – their handshake was better than a contract drawn up by the cleverest lawyers in the world.

Going places

Kim and Flow had hacked out new pathways.

Clea had well and truly leapt.

Only the principal was left, restless in her pond.
Out of space, perhaps almost out of time,
she lay in shallow waters, alone and gasping.

Kim was absorbing the coursework like a thirsty sponge, taking full advantage of all the college had to offer whilst the opportunity presented itself. The photography department had a top of the range digital camera with tripod and lighting that they let him borrow and the IT department answered any questions rising about how to build a website.

His official course was business planning, strategy and management, but the extra energy to do it all came easily, now that he had a goal in his sights.

Flow was getting up at four thirty every day to get the hours in with his cabbing. Starting so early meant he got airport jobs, which paid the most. He took people home from their holidays and business trips after long haul flights into Heathrow, enabling him to pocket a good wad of cash before the unpredictable bits and pieces came trickling in.

He would knock off at two thirty in the afternoon with a ten-hour day under his belt. After getting some kip, he would pick Kim up from college at five. They would eat an early dinner, digest for a bit, then set about decorating.

Topped up with cash from drug sales, they had a pretty good income to bankroll their venture, after Flow's initial cash injection from his savings.

The first thing they'd done was to knock the back of the flat into one big room, tearing the dirty old kitchen out. They had rented a skip to chuck the debris into, including the garden junk left by the previous tenants.

Glass doors went in across the back wall looking onto the garden, after which they set about turning the new inside space into a kitchen, eating and entertainment area.

Using good lighting, slick kitchen units, a couple of well-chosen sofas, entertainment system and contemporary-looking rubberised floor, they had made an incredible living space.

The rubber floor climbed part of the wall to form a sort of easy to wash basketball bin area with various holes for the rubbish: paper, cans and so on, and some choice spray painting, in that patch of the room.

It was Flow's 'tag' for that particular project, the detail they had decided would set their work apart from everybody else's. They had already spent many happy times throwing and flicking things into the various bins from the different spots in the room.

'Of course you can do it.' Flow looked at Kim uncertainly and surveyed the fillets of fish that they had picked up from the market on the way home from college, suspiciously. He prodded the potatoes with a fork. They were nearly done and ready to mash. 'Come on, Flow, put them in the pan, unless you want sushi for dinner,' urged Kim.

With a surge of action, Flow seized the spatula and shuffled one of the fillets into the hot frying pan.

'That's it. Now hold it down for a bit, not long – easy.'

Kim had been happy to teach Flow to cook when he'd asked, careful not to make a big thing out of it. People always saw Flow as an easy-going, carefree joker but Kim knew that he ran much deeper than that. He could see that this was a big

The Frog Theory

deal for some reason, and the reason didn't matter unless Flow wanted to tell him.

Just as they finished their last (successful) mouthful the doorbell rang. Kim jogged down the hall to answer it, and found Jackie standing there.

Jackie had moved back onto the estate with her parents after the split and was none too pleased when she hadn't been able to track Flow down.

News that Kim had knocked Ryan out had soon got around and Jackie had been to see Ryan, chastising him heavily for dobbing her in, denying the affair to anyone who would listen.

She had rung Flow's parents, begging them to tell her where Flow was, pleading innocence. Of course, they had remained loyal to Flow so eventually, in desperation, she had taken time off from Boots, claiming sickness to stalk the cab office, hoping Flow still worked there, and had eventually tracked him to Doria Road.

'You're not welcome here,' said Kim, moving to close the door. Jackie was too quick, jamming it hastily with her foot. Kim's heart sank to his feet – was Flow going to go back to her again? She looked amazing and she could be persuasive.

'Problem?' Flow asked, joining him.

'See for yourself,' said Kim.

Flow opened the door wide, uncharacteristically calm and still. Kim stood slightly behind him, the space in the doorway not big enough for them both.

'You!' Jackie managed eventually, the sight of him looking so well and happy, no longer under her control, affecting her deeply. Her plans to act like a wrongly accused victim deserted her as pure fury took over.

'The nerve,' she blurted. 'After everything I've done for you, you ungrateful git.'

'I've got nothing to say to you,' said Flow, quietly but clearly.

Well done, Flow, thought Kim, readying himself for whatever was to come.

'You blinking idiot, Flow, how *dare* you believe that lying twit

Ryan over me, how *dare* you? Don't you know he's wanted me for ages? Say *anything* to split us up, he would, Flow, anything. You're so fucking thick, ruining everything we had, all our plans...nobody was ever happier than we were, you don't get things that special twice in life. And you...' She redirected her wrath at Kim. 'You're just as bad, egging him on, never could handle Flow loving me, always had it in for us, you did, you're an idiot too.'

She tapped her foot a few times while she looked expectantly from one to the other.

'Well, if we're both idiots what are you doing here?' Flow said calmly, her power over him non-existent now.

That stumped her. With no verbal retort left she lost physical control and hurled herself at Flow, madly scratching, pummelling, and hysterical. It put Kim in mind of a frenzied cat and he thought how apt the expression 'cat fight' was in certain situations.

Jackie's fingernails were digging into Flow's neck and drawing blood, so rather than dwelling on the comparison, he grabbed her shoulders firmly and pulled as hard as he could, giving Flow the chance to push her away. They literally bundled her out onto the street and slammed the door.

'I'll get you, Frank Young, you see if I don't!' she yelled through the letter box before stomping away.

'Fuuuuuk,' said Flow, doubling over from her punches.

'Let's get decorating,' said Kim, making his way back to the living room, leaving Flow to collect himself in the hall for a couple of minutes.

Clea had decided to take a chance on a flat-share in Paris, rather than an apartment on her own, which had been her original preference. Charlie had nagged her to death on the subject, he simply wouldn't budge. She had half expected she would find Flash in her suitcase if she refused and she was glad he *had* pushed her because she had ended up making a good friend.

The Frog Theory

Her name was Melissa, also from London, doing the same course, the full 'Acting in English' programme, which included theatre exercises, workshops on imagination and senses, improvisation and more.

Melissa was in many ways opposite to Clea, which could make for good friendship combinations and she laughed easily, which helped to lighten Clea up.

Charlie had insisted that Clea take some hypnotherapy sessions, he said it would be good for her self-esteem, that anger would only get her so far before it destroyed her. What anger? Who was she kidding, she had compartmentalised her experiences and although she felt physically safe being so far away from Hugo, going by her father's surname, rather than his – if she even touched upon the subject, her mind felt like it immediately tuned into a radio transmission of his hatred for her.

Hypnotherapy was something she could do over the phone and it was helping to create new thought processes – NLP, it was called: Neuro-Linguistic Programming. She had been given scripts that she could play on her headphones and sometimes, if she had problems sleeping or was troubled by nightmares, she would play them and it helped her to tune out Hugo, to balance her once again. It also gave her basic life-skills such as eat well, sleep well, look after yourself.

Melissa was refreshingly childish, the youngest of four children, 'an evening star,' her parents called her, for there was a fair gap between her and her elder siblings. She would randomly start a pillow fight or get the giggles over something quite silly but her laughter was contagious and she always put Clea at ease.

'What are you doing?' said Clea as she chowed down a bowl of soup, glimpsing Melissa out of the corner of her eye.

'I'm seeing how long I can stand on one leg,' explained Melissa, concentrating hard. She was wearing a fluffy dressing gown, ridiculous bath cap and huge slippers in the shape of teddy bears.

'Well there's soup on the stove, if you want it?'

'Thanks,' said Melissa. 'I'm taking a shower first.' They were going to a local bar that evening, a typical way to spend their time. Some of their course mates would be there and they would probably have a few drinks and be home by midnight. All of them, without exception, took their studies very seriously and worked extremely hard.

'Okay,' said Clea, wondering what she was going to wear. 'Are you going in jeans or something smarter?'

'Dunno,' said Melissa, bringing one finger steadily to her nose, crossing her eyes in the process. 'I haven't decided.'

'I think I'll wear jeans,' said Clea, getting up to clear her bowl away. 'It's cold.' She shivered, thinking she may pair the jeans with her new bomber jacket.

The course was to last for a year, after which they would return to London and attend an International Dance Academy, unless one or both of them got offered work before then, but either way they had decided they would share again. Clea's natural talent had already been noticed and the chances that she would get work were high.

'*Laisse aller, la nuit est jeune,*' Melissa announced, reappearing from her bedroom in some kind of glamorous trouser-suit, her hair dramatically styled. Her French was much better than Clea's.

'Yes, the night *is* young,' translated Clea. 'But what about your soup?'

Melissa had a bad habit of skipping meals.

'I'm not really that hungry.' She went to put her coat on.

'You should line your tummy, you haven't eaten since breakfast.' Clea was already spooning soup into a bowl for her.

Melissa begrudgingly left the coat and sat at the table. Clea tucked a tea towel into the top of her trouser-suit and laughed.

'Okay, okay,' said Melissa. 'I'll eat.' She soon found out how hungry she was and was grateful for the friendly nudge. 'Thanks.' She shot Clea one of her endearing looks of appreciation.

The Frog Theory

Clea relaxed. In many ways she treated Melissa as she imagined she might treat a younger sister, if she had one.

Dear Diary,

I thought Hugo would calm down once Clea was gone but if anything, it's made him even more mad. I tried to reason with him, said surely it was a good thing he didn't have to worry about her anymore but that muscle in his cheek hammered faster than usual and I knew he was angry again.

Ever since the car debacle he has kept a baseball bat by the bed and he gets up throughout the night to look out of the window, pacing up and down like a crazed madman. I didn't think life could get worse, but it has.

Testing natural chemistry

The year flew – college had come to an end for Kim in London, and Clea's Paris course had finished, too.

As soon as she landed in England, however, the uneasy feeling that Hugo was going to jump out at her returned. Staying with Melissa's family whilst they searched for a flat to share and worked out their next career moves helped – but the fearful feeling that he was out to get her never completely subsided.

The rules Melissa's parents laid down were pretty easy – be back by midnight or stay out! She could work with that.

Doria Road was looking like something out of a contemporary design magazine and Kim and Flow were enjoying their last few weeks there. All photo shoots were completed and they had uploaded the final images to the website. They were incredibly proud of their hard work.

It would soon be time to hand over to Leigh as agreed. Neither of them wanted to return to their homes on the estate – doing that would be a disappointing step backwards. They had got used to their freedom from respective family and friends, it felt like they were on the right path and they needed to keep walking.

The plan was to buy somewhere, a first step on the property ladder, but they were a long way off that so they struck on the idea of renting a garage. It would be cheap and they could make one liveable fairly easily, as long as it had plumbing for them to secretly put in a loo and shower-room, then they could save hard for the deposit on a flat.

The Frog Theory

* * *

The principal had presented her usual inspirational farewell speech to the class, expecting Kim to come back, but he had simply walked out into the world with the rest of her protégés. She felt an intense pull of sadness, and of loss. He had brought her close to what it was like to feel once more, and to lose that precious fragment, meant losing the ability to find the place inside of her that so desperately longed to be fixed.

But Kim had made a note of her home address long ago when he had seen it on the letters strewn across her desk, and he figured now he wasn't a student anymore, he would simply go to her house sometime and take his chances on whether she would be there or not.

'Kim,' she said in surprise, finding him on her doorstep. She felt all the connections he sparked in her return with a heavenly *whooshing*, and suppressed the urge to fling herself into his arms like a love-struck teenager.

Inconveniently, he found himself struck dumb. *Wing it*, had been the plan, but *wing it* was bringing absolutely nothing to mind.

'Come in,' she found herself suggesting. 'Have a drink with me.'

Her house was huge and full of antique furniture. Funny, Kim had imagined her in young, modern surroundings.

She led him into the drawing room.

'Whisky? Wine? Beer?' she asked, wondering what she was playing at. 'Something soft?'

Beer.

The room had a high ceiling and a gas log open fire that looked so real, Kim had to fiddle with it before he'd believe it wasn't. Just the sort of thing Flow would have done – they were spending way too much time together.

The principal came back and handed him the drink. He sat

on a chesterfield and swigged his beer out of the bottle, rather than using the glass she had provided.

He managed to find his voice.

'This place...I thought you'd live somewhere modern.'

'My mother gave it to us...part of the legacy – family money.' She explained further. 'Mustard.'

'Mustard?' questioned Kim.

'Yes!' She smiled at his look of confusion. 'One of the oldest existing food brands, started in 1814...our family fortune is built on it – mustard.'

'Right,' he said, once more struck inconveniently dumb. He didn't know much about the ways of rich folk. Mustard. He guessed if you sold enough of it worldwide, that would be a lot of money, yes.

'So, what brings you here, Kim?'

'I didn't say thank you...or goodbye,' he began. 'And I did want to say thank you...and goodbye,' he added lamely, mentally kicking himself as usual for sounding so inarticulate in her presence.

'Well, that's nice of you.' She looked at him in cool amusement from her armchair, sipping her whisky. 'It was a pleasure to have you at the college, Kim. What are you up to now?'

His plan for renting a garage to live in suddenly seemed very silly and immature, so instead he blurted out, 'I missed you.' Like that was somehow less immature.

Natural chemistry. *Bugger!* thought the principal. Kim was not a student anymore, that was true. And she wasn't the type of person who would care what people thought about her. But it was somehow very wrong, even if she couldn't exactly pinpoint why.

'Kim, you know there will never be anything more than friendship between us, don't you?'

The usual cool of her voice was compromised and Kim was acutely aware of it. He took in her body language and was sure, for the first time, that she shared his desire, although she was

The Frog Theory

trying hard not to show it, and his nerves were gone. He walked towards her and dropped to his knees at her feet.

'Every time I see you it feels like this,' he said, looking up at her.

She raised a cool eyebrow.

'It'll pass.' She willed her heart to slow down.

He began to kiss his way upwards, completely at ease, he knew for sure he was good at this.

'Have you nearly finished?' she asked – but found she couldn't move as the sensation pulled her in.

He went slowly higher, pushing her skirt up, his hands dwarfing her slender frame. 'We shouldn't...I shouldn't,' she began breathlessly as he gently pulled her into the moment. It felt to her like she was taking advantage of her position of authority – she was sure there was a mutual type of transference taking place, causing the compelling magnetism, which she should immediately remove herself from and analyse.

But her body was responding warmly to its first human contact in so long that her reservations were fast disappearing. She willed it once again to stop but she was so sick of restricting herself and so desperate for a real person to touch her that she could no longer fight.

He pulled her roughly towards him so that she was hanging over the chair, her skirt riding up around her waist, her legs around his neck and, at last, she was free of conscious thought.

He didn't stop until he was sure she had finished her orgasm. Her breathing began to slow and he pushed her gently back on the chair, dizzy with restraining his own pressing needs. She came to her senses and got up, snatched her ripped knickers from the floor and pushed her hair out of her face.

'My God,' she said. 'I know better than this.' She stalked out of the room and he heard her go upstairs and slam a door.

The principal had locked herself in the bathroom and was looking at herself in the mirror with her hand over her mouth. *What had she done?* She hadn't had sex with anything but her vibrator since finding Mike in bed with her sister. Raw and long forgotten emotions were resurfacing and the face that stared back at her was far from repentant, as she would have hoped. No, it was deliciously naughty and radiant, eager for more.

Kim knocked on the bathroom door and she opened it, peering around.

'You have to go,' she begged. 'Pleeeeease...?'

'Okay,' said Kim, sensing that he had knocked down some mother-fucker of a wall. He smiled.

She found herself giving him a huge smile in return, hiding coyly behind the door like a kid, as he disappeared down the stairs, out of the house.

She breathed a contented sigh and got into the shower, humming to herself, singing a little bit of Abba into the loofa. She felt a strange sense of being here now, under the hot water, with no thought of tomorrow. Relaxed and happy for the first time in as long as she could tangibly remember.

Why don't you join us for dinner?

Clea felt an inexplicable compulsion to return to Fulham to look at the house she had so dramatically exited from; a compulsion which only increased as the days passed. Did she want to see her mum? She didn't know. Her fear of Hugo was at times paralysing, did she want to confront him?

She guessed that looking at the house might be a little like looking under a bandage to see how well a wound was healing. Yes, that was exactly it, she must go. The answers would come.

As she stood there she took a few breaths to calm herself. She had changed significantly inside and out. She still wished that things had been different but her new life excited her and that excitement superseded the sadness of the past. She had done the right thing.

She had done the right thing, she thought once more. Relief swept through her. Hugo's Porsche was nowhere to be seen. With a shudder she hurried away. The feeling that Hugo wished her harm was even stronger here, almost like an electrical current emitting hate, making her feel physically sick.

She ducked down Doria Road towards the main street where she could jump on a bus or grab a taxi back to the life she had so diligently built.

She quickened her step just as Flow came out of the flat on a cigarette-run, bringing them face to face, almost in collision.

'My God,' said Clea, her face breaking into a smile. 'I don't believe it, small world or what – blows me away.'

'Clea!' said Flow, stepping back and returning the smile. 'How long's it been...a year? More? Where did you get to?'

They walked to the shop together and chatted without pause about all the things they had each been up to and Flow found himself asking her to join them for dinner at the Italian restaurant him and Kim were going to that evening.

Clea was apprehensive at the idea of seeing Kim again, her ego had been badly bruised, yet she yearned to show that she had listened to him, that she was grateful – *that she had finally jumped out of boiling water.*

So, she accepted and soon found herself walking into the flat.

'You'll never believe who I found on the way to the shop,' Flow called happily from the hall.

They walked through to the main room at the back where Kim was leisurely stretched on the sofa, mindlessly flicking through the TV channels.

'Wow!' said Clea, looking around. 'Absolutely, completely... *amazing* place.'

The hairs on the back of Kim's neck rose at the sound of her voice, sort of forgotten yet strangely familiar – he swivelled around.

'It's Clea,' stated Flow, needlessly.

Kim took in the amber of her glance and felt his stomach twist. Clea had changed. She looked relaxed and happy and was not hiding behind her hair anymore. And he was every bit as attracted to her as he had been before.

'You remember each other, don't you?' said Flow.

'How could anyone ever forget Kim, how are you?' said Clea, with false bravado.

Whatever connection they had preciously shared seemed to be all around them like an uncomfortable, unfinished subject. She was beginning to think she had made a mistake.

Kim managed a bit of a smile. At least, he hoped it looked like a smile. Clea hadn't replied to the message he'd left on her bedroom windowsill. In his mind, she had rejected him.

The Frog Theory

He did not realise that she had run away from home before finding it.

Maybe she was going to want Flow and if that was the case, he was going to have to accept it. Magnanimously.

'Let's go and eat, I'm starving,' said Flow. 'We're going to the Italian place down the road,' he said, for Clea's benefit. 'Now that we can finally stop spending money on the business for five fucking seconds.'

He explained that they had finished renovating the flat and that their website was also finished so they could afford to go and eat out tonight.

The place was small and packed, and there was a large table of people along one side, chatting loudly.

'Great vibe,' said Clea, trying not to imagine Hugo walking past and seeing her through the window.

They ordered quickly; pasta carbonara for Flow, meatballs for Kim and seafood salad for Clea.

Try as he might, and he tried very hard, Kim could not relax. Every time he looked at Clea or joined in with the conversation he was paranoid that Flow would pick up on his feelings for her. In the end, he zoned out and thought about what he needed to do next to link their website to the search engines as he chomped through his food.

Clea took his aloofness personally and it flung her back to memories of bad times.

The Brogue Slamming Against Her Head.
Insubordinate Bitch.

The unpleasant telescope to the past, put her on edge, but luckily Flow did most of the talking and the food was delicious, which helped her keep difficult memories at bay. A little wine added to the good feelings – just her with the vino, a carafe – Kim and Flow drank lager, reminding her of the party where she had first met them, leaning against the bar with their pints.

'There are places in Thailand where the girls shoot darts out of their, you know...' Flow waggled his eyebrows ridiculously and Clea giggled, nearly spitting her mouthful of food over the table. 'You must have heard of them? No? Anyway, there was this underground replica of it in Soho we all went to for a laugh and our mate Pat got hit, right in the temple, didn't he, Kim? We all ended up in A & E.' Kim didn't contribute. 'And Ryan pulled one of the nurses...' nudged Flow further, looking at Kim expectantly.

The mention of Ryan momentarily brought Kim to the conversation but he was soon gone again. 'I'll just talk to you, I think,' said Flow to Clea.

'Suits me,' she said, with a sideways glance at Kim who was chomping through his meatballs like some sort of machine.

'Oh my God, what you did to Hugo's car. You did do that, right? I saw you...sitting on the roof. How could I have forgotten to ask you about it and to thank you, until now?'

She'd left home after that.

The Brogue Slamming Against Her Head.
Insubordinate Bitch.

Fuck – off – bad – memories. She instructed her mind firmly, concentrating as hard as she could on listening to what was going on inside the room rather than inside her head.

'That was Flow,' said Kim, proudly, putting his knife and fork to one side, suddenly back in the conversation after finishing his meatballs.

Maybe he was just hungry, thought Clea. 'He can do anything,' said Kim. 'I've never seen anyone as good – he should have gone to art school. His mum and dad tried to make him but he wouldn't leave the estate.'

'Yeah...that was more about hating being institutionalised, though. School was never my thing. I just get this mood and I can do it – paint, spray stuff. But only when I feel like it and

The Frog Theory

only for a laugh, I could never do it as a job but like this, with Kim – it doesn't *feel* like a job, it's more kinda natural.'

They explained that the rubberised bin area at Doria Road was the creative 'tag' for that particular project and told Clea about how often they had played at chucking things into it. 'It's addictive, I swear – come and try.'

'Have you ever been caught? While you were spraying, I mean?' asked Clea curiously.

'Nah. Been chased, though...like, we got chased the night we did the ice cream van car, didn't we, Kim?'

But he was gone again. *What was it with him tonight?* Flow couldn't work it out.

Kim's behaviour was triggering Clea's negative emotions and they were starting to crowd out everything else. *I can't stop them anymore,* she thought. *Kim doesn't like me, nobody likes me when it really comes down to it, and why should they? What is there to like? I'm just a stupid, idiotic little girl who'll never get anywhere in life, not really.*

She found herself missing what Flow was saying entirely for at least ten minutes while her mind taunted her, Hugo's horrible voice disguised as her own. So loud, so insistent and so determined to be heard.

Flow clapped his hands together.

'Dessert, anyone?'

Kim gave a long yawn and gazed longingly towards the door. He had started something with the principal just this very day and now Clea had popped up out of the blue causing feelings that were sending him all over the place, he needed to get out of here. He flung his bank card on the table, about to ask for the bill so that he could make his escape as the waiter approached with a dessert trolley.

'Dessert trolley. Retro,' commented Flow, looking with appreciation at the display.

The waiter described the dessert options whilst Kim rudely drummed his fingers on the table and looked distractedly around the restaurant.

Clea felt her anger rise like boiling milk.

'Excuse me,' she said to the waiter, picking up a large strawberry gateau.

'No, no...we sell it by the slice, you don't take the whole thing!' he exclaimed. *Some people could be such pigs*, he thought.

'I'm not going to eat it,' said Clea, her face alight with mischief. 'Kiiiim,' she called, and as soon as he looked at her she squidged the cake soundly into his surprised, glum face.

There.

That stopped everything, Hugo's stupid voice included.

The people at the surrounding tables stared at Kim as the bulk of the impressive pudding made its gloopy way down his front. The big party were now drinking grappa and seemed the most interested.

A moment passed and Kim seized a gooey-looking lemon meringue pie, plonking it onto Clea's head like a pillar box hat.

'*Mon dieu*,' cried the waiter, throwing his hands into the air.

'Hey, that's French, not Italian, even I know that!' said Flow as Clea swiped a chocolate gateau and plied Kim with it. 'Wo-ah wo-ah wo-ah!' said Flow, jumping to his feet. The waiter scuttled off to the kitchen screaming something in Italian.

A bread roll hit Flow hard on the ear. 'Who threw that?' he asked the restaurant in general, looking around – it had become alive with flying bread rolls and other items of food.

Some people had begun to cheer and whoop, taking photos and films on their phones, whilst a spattering of more sober onlookers sat aghast.

'Stop throwing my food!' screamed the manager, running into the middle of the restaurant, brandishing a giant pepper mill.

'You heard the man,' shouted Flow indignantly. 'What are we? Three-year-olds?' With that, he picked up the salt pot and expertly chucked it into a water jug on the grappa table, where it made a satisfying *sploosh*, splashing water into the face of the person he suspected of throwing the bread roll.

Clea made her way around the tables and out of the door.

The Frog Theory

Kim chased her down the street with Flow following slightly later, the manger fast closing in.

The poor guy came huffing and puffing after them, still brandishing the pepper mill above his head.

Being fit as she was, Clea managed to put on an extra burst of speed and jumped onto a passing bus.

'I'll get you for this!' Kim yelled, shaking his fist at the number 22 as it whizzed off up the King's Road. He wouldn't have had a clue what to do if he'd have caught her, but it felt good to shout it, anyway.

In a matter of seconds Flow caught up with Kim and they continued to run from the manager, still in pursuit, but fast losing ground.

Eventually they came to a stop down Bells Alley, safe.

'Do you know how random and lucky it was that I bumped into Clea like that, do you have any fucking idea?' yelled Flow. Kim hadn't seen him so angry since he had accused him of trying to get hold of Jackie. 'I *still* haven't got her number and she doesn't go to her mum's any more, you absolute – DICK,' said Flow, full of fury. He foraged for his phone and dialled the cab company he worked for. 'Plus – I've got her purse, she left it on the table in the restaurant, but I was in kind of a hurry and your card's still there...by the way.'

He had narrowly missed being clonked on the head with the menacing pepper mill.

He waited for his cab company to pick up the phone.

'Then she'll come to the flat to get her purse, won't she?' reasoned Kim, hoping that was true and wondering what was going to happen, now that the restaurant had his bank card. 'I'm sorry...but she's the one who threw the fucking... strawberry fucking...cake thing.' He struggled for the words.

'You were being a shit – no, not you,' he said to the controller who had answered his call. 'I need you to radio all drivers in the SW area and ask them to look for a girl, about five foot ten, blondish, covered in food. What? No, I'm not joking. There's been a food fight, just do me a favour and put the call out,' said Flow, increasingly frustrated. 'And call me straight away if you hear anything,' he finished, pressing end and returning his attention to Kim. 'What the fuck was up with you?' he said, quizzical.

Kim sighed one of his big sighs.

'I'm sorry,' he said eventually, shrugging his shoulders. 'Really...I am,' he added, when Flow showed no signs of responding. Flow's body language softened.

Ordinarily, Kim would have been absolutely honest but he didn't want to say that he had some seriously confusing emotions about Clea. It would spoil things for Flow – he didn't want that.

'I just...after the Jackie thing I'm scared for you...for our friendship,' he put forward, feeling like a real shit. 'I thought I'd be okay but when it came to it I just felt...threatened.'

There, that was kind of true. Flow clapped him on the back.

'I get it,' he said. 'And I appreciate it.' He pulled a pack of cigarettes from his pocket and offered one to Kim – a peace offering that Kim felt he didn't really deserve. 'All I'm saying is you'd better pray we find her – 'cos that's the first girl I've liked in a very long time.' He picked a strawberry covered in chocolate sauce off Kim's top and popped it into his mouth. 'S'really nice,' he said thoughtfully, before lighting his cigarette.

Meanwhile, the bus conductor eyed Clea suspiciously, nervous of a passenger who looked like they were covered in...was it pudding? Presently he asked her very politely, from a distance, to get off his bus.

Since Clea didn't have enough money for the fare, her purse nowhere to be found, she hopped off quietly, the gaze of many judgemental eyes burning into her back. She was mortified, alone, and quite a long way up the Kings Road. She had her phone in her pocket, but it had run out of battery, so her best option was probably to walk back to Doria Road looking like some kind of crazy tiramisu swamp monster to try and get her purse back.

The Frog Theory

Cursing her stupid temper, she was fighting back tears when a cab pulled up beside her.

'You a friend of Flow's?' the driver asked. 'Claire?'

'Yes,' she said. 'Clea, actually – how do you know?'

'Never mind just...' he stopped mid-sentence to stare at her in amazement. 'What the?' he began. 'Is that chocolate cake all down you?'

'Partly.' She shrugged apologetically.

'Just...wait,' he said, phone in hand, hazards on. 'I've found your girl, Claire.'

Yes! Thought Flow triumphantly, high-fiving Kim. 'And unless she's prepared to sit on top of the car and hang onto the roof-rack, there's no way I'm taking her anywhere covered in *that*.'

After a while and a few 'yeps' and 'nopes' he hung up and handed Clea some money. He pointed to a late-night supermarket not far off.

'Go in there and get some bin bags to sit on.'

'Thank you,' Clea replied meekly, bracing herself for the sort of looks she just knew she was going to get in the supermarket. Tears started to flow freely down her face. How could she have got herself in such a mess? She was better that this nowadays and she was so cross with herself.

'Oy!' called the driver, taking pity and beckoning her back. 'Just wait by the car and don't let it get towed – I'll get the bags.' She sniffed gratefully and tried her best to collect herself.

They were soon pulling up next to Flow and Kim who were sitting on the pavement waiting for them down a side road.

'Look at the state of you,' said the driver, handing Kim the roll of bin bags. Kim had taken his top off but there was not a lot he could do about his hair or his bottom half – even his shoes were full of cream and sauce. 'Worse than her,' he said, pointing at Clea, who had stayed in the car. 'You'd best not trifle with me,' he said with a chuckle once they were all in and he had started to pull away from the kerb.

Fiona Mordaunt

Flow raised his eyes to heaven.

'Not funny,' muttered Clea.

Back at the flat they paid him extra for his trouble and stood in the hall, not wanting to get goo all over the place and very much at an uncomfortable stalemate.

'So,' said Flow in the end, 'anyone fancy a cup of coffee to go with that dessert?' He looked at them hopefully, praying for one of them to pacify the charged atmosphere.

Kim looked apologetically at Clea, who didn't meet his eye. 'I guess that'll teach *me* to be rude.' Flow wanted to cry with relief that Kim had pulled out of his strop. 'Just looking out for my friend,' he continued. 'His last girl did a bit of a number on him...overprotective, what can I say? Forgive me.'

'I...' began Clea. 'You...' she tried again. 'Me!' she gave up for a moment. 'You shouldn't be sorry, it's *me* who should be sorry. I can't believe I did that, I'm *so* sorry. I mean...throwing food! I just don't know...who was that? I guess I must be really fucked up...I just...it was seeing my mum's house again, feeling all...fucked up, I...oversensitive, just...'

'Would you like to go and get a shower?' Kim interrupted, desperate to save her from her nervous gibberish.

Clea nodded gratefully and Flow showed her to the bathroom. He gave her a towel and some of his clothes, which would be too big but at least *clean*.

It was too late for Clea to go back to Melissa's – midnight curfew – so it was agreed that she would stay at Doria Road and go back in the morning. She charged her phone enough to text Melissa, so that she did not worry.

Flow showered last as he was the least affected, leaving Clea and Kim in awkward silence, sitting on opposite sofas.

'I just need to ask you one thing – why didn't you reply to my letter?'

'Letter?' questioned Clea, blankly. 'What letter?'

'Come on,' said Kim. 'The letter I left you in the beer bottle, on your bedroom windowsill, you must have seen it?'

'I didn't,' said Clea honestly. 'I never stayed...I...that frog theory thing...thank you.' It was too hard to say that she had run away so she left it like that and hoped it conveyed how grateful she was. 'What did it say?'

'It doesn't matter now,' said Kim. 'But it's good to know you didn't get it...explains why you never called.'

Kim had asked her to call? She had been so convinced that he hated her. 'Look, it's so long ago I don't really remember what it said, now – I upset you and I wanted to say sorry, is all.' He looked away from her puzzled expression, too endearing. She didn't push further, and he liked that.

'Anyway, I'm going to bed,' he stated.

Clea wasn't sure whether Flow was expecting romance but avoided the possibility by offering to sleep on the sofa, stressing how tired she was after everything that had happened. Flow said she could have his bed and he could sleep on the sofa, sensing for sure that nothing was going to happen between them that night, but she had been insistent, accepting his giant T-shirt, which was like a dress on her. She now lay in the dark with her eyes wide open.

Would the bottle with the letter in it still be there?

And if so, what did it say? Maybe it explained why Kim didn't find her attractive enough to kiss, she cringed at the thought.

It had been such a huge deal for her at the time, shattering her confidence, that she felt she had to know.

Quietly she made her way to the front door, slipped on her shoes, and left it on the latch.

It was around four thirty in the morning by now and she was soon in the garden of her old house in Alderville Road, looking up at the bedroom that had been hers for so many years. By quietly moving the garden table beneath the window she was able to stand with a stick and poke around in the ivy.

Sure enough, tangled amongst the leaves, nestled a beer bottle.

Her heart began to beat faster.

She placed one of the garden chairs on the table, then by

balancing on it precariously she was just able to nudge the beer bottle free with the stick and send it falling towards her.

She caught it neatly in her hands, replaced all the furniture and made her escape.

Back at Doria Road she found the door as she had left it, snuck back in, and closed it quietly behind her before tiptoeing back to the sofa.

But getting the note out of the bottle was no easy task. It had fallen right in. First of all, she shook the bottle upside down, hoping it would slide out. Not a chance.

The roll of the note had expanded to fit snuggly around the inside of the bottle. Next, she tried to reach it by sticking her little finger inside with the bottle upside down, wiggling it like a demented worm.

No joy. Finger too short, not even touching the edge of the paper. She tried her ring finger. It got stuck, only coming free after a forceful jerk.

POP!

'Shhhhhhh!' she scolded herself in the dark.

She realised that the only way she was going to get at the note was to smash the bottle. Too noisy. She was going to have to wait, burning with curiosity all the while.

When daylight broke she left the flat. She had shoved her clothes, her purse and the bottle into a Sainsbury's bag she had found under the sink, leaving a note to say thank you, promising to return the clothes.

Dressed in Flow's tracksuit bottoms, enormous on her, twinned with one of his outsized hoodies, she made her way back to Melissa's, knowing that she could not reasonably knock on the door until at least 8am, but pleased to be able to travel whilst there weren't too many people to see her strange appearance.

Now, where and how to smash the bottle? She would put it in a bag and smash it with a hammer, or rolling pin, she thought.

The Frog Theory

Then there was no guarantee that the note would even be legible, after all that effort, it was so very frustrating.

Melissa's Mum was busy whizzing up some kind of crazy health shake when she finally knocked on the door, and didn't even notice Clea's strange appearance, so she slunk off upstairs to change into her own clothes.

Then as soon as the kitchen was free, and the rest of the house otherwise distracted, she went and found the kit she needed to finally break the bottle.

Trembling slightly, she placed it in a bag, just as she had imagined, took it into the garden and gave it a good *whack* with the rolling pin.

The letter was free.

She plucked it carefully from the broken pieces of glass and unrolled it.

I really wanted to kiss you but couldn't. Let me explain, I've looked for you everywhere but it's like you've disappeared. Call me and if you're in trouble I'll come and get you. I can't stop thinking about you. Kim X

Clea stared at the note, Kim's phone number clearly printed at the bottom: 'really wanted to kiss you but couldn't.' All that time she had ached and all that time the letter had been just there, sitting in the ivy.

Food fight goes viral

Locals were shocked when a food fight broke out between a young lady and two young gentlemen in a usually quiet Italian restaurant in Fulham...

'Must be something wrong with my phone – fifty-two missed calls,' Kim said to Flow as he flicked the kettle on for another cup of tea. He couldn't bring himself to ask how his night with Clea had gone. He assumed they had 'got it together' and this was a good distraction.

Flow studied his phone too, with a furrowed brow. 'Something's going on,' Kim stated, flicking through his texts and missed calls as the kettle offered its comforting purrs. 'I think we should take a look at YouTube. Seems we might be famous.'

It was true. The restaurant had been able to get their identities/website from the bank cards and it had gone viral, capturing the imagination of people everywhere.

There was a pretty coherent film of the fight on YouTube, taken on someone's mobile phone in the restaurant, and even an extremely comical snippet of the chase, including the manager brandishing the giant pepper mill. The films were attracting thousands of hits already.

'First, I'm going to catch you, then I'm going to sprinkle you with pepper', someone had tweeted.

Papers and all sorts of other people had been calling Kim, hoping for an interview and more information about what had caused the fight to begin.

The Frog Theory

More exciting, there were business enquiries. Free – national – advertising. (Well, apart from the big chunk of money the Italian restaurant would surely expect, they would have to smooth things over with them somehow, but still.) This was heaven-sent.

Dear Diary,
Hugo has found Clea. I saw him on the computer watching her in a bizarre food fight, he didn't even notice me. I could tell by the set of his shoulders how angry he was, he hit the desk with his fist and said that he would kill the insubordinate bitch, that he would find her.

Clea had been mulling over Kim's letter. Now she knew exactly why he had refused to kiss her that night by the river – because of Flow. Flow had been the one to ask her out, she had just been too blind to consider that he liked her in *that way* because of his engagement to Jackie.

For whatever reason, Flow had been unable to make it and Kim had gone in his place, simply planning to get her number but of course…she had slammed the front door of her house before he got the chance, begging him to take her out with them.

It sent a warm surge of comfort through her, swiftly followed by panic when she thought about the situation now. She didn't want to cause a rift in Kim and Flow's friendship. She also felt terrified by the way she had been so quickly thrown back to the past. She had no idea how Kim felt now and even if he still liked her, the destructive behaviour he seemed to unleash in her was manic.

No more dabbling with this thing that had the ability to send her off the rails so easily, she counselled herself, as she approached Doria Road. She had a career to concentrate on, now; real friends, too, for the first time in her life. She had decided to return the clothes that day to get it over with; she simply must make sure that she looked after herself.

* * *

She was surprised by the enthusiastic welcome she received from Kim, who quickly answered the door after the bell rang.

'How did you know to come? Did you hear? Did you see it?'

'What? No! I just brought the clothes back,' she stammered as Kim led her to the main living space and sat her in front of the computer.

'We're famous,' he announced. 'Watch yourself on TV.'

Clea sat, bewildered as the clips began to play.

'Oh – my – *God*,' she said.

'There's more.' Kim clicked onto the chase with the giant pepper mill. 'This is fucking great for all of us, Clea – we've got loads of business enquiries. Your information needs to be on there quick, while people are still interested, and we've got to give them more of a story to keep it going…so what's our story?' He looked expectantly from Flow to Clea. 'Why did the food fight start?'

'Well,' began Flow, 'you were being a shit – Clea got cross and lobbed a strawberry gateau at you.'

'That's about the size of it,' said Clea, nodding her agreement.

When put like that, she sounded like much less of a freak, it was hugely comforting.

'Oh, come on,' said Kim. 'Where's your imagination?'

'Well, what would you say?' said Flow.

Kim grabbed his laptop and started to type, reading aloud as he went.

'Talented and sought-after actress, Clea Scott-Davis (see Linkedin profile) dining with two friends who own a new contemporary design company (see website) lost her cool when a disagreement broke out between herself and fellow diner, Kim Carter. None of them will say what the disagreement was over but we are hoping for an interview, so watch this space.'

'Okay…but who will write that for us and where?'

'Errrr…one of the many journalists that have contacted us, perhaps?' said Kim, thinking that was blindingly obvious.

The Frog Theory

'And we can say something fucking whacked like the argument was over what biscuits are best to dunk in your tea, you know – something that makes people go, *what? It was over that?*,' said Flow, warming up now. 'Like you say chocolate Hobnobs—'

'I would never say chocolate Hobnobs,' interrupted Kim. 'They crumble too much, make the tea taste like shit – everybody knows that.'

Clea concealed a smile as she listened to them banter backwards and forwards.

They spent some time linking her in with her profile pictures and CV, then Flow took her home, leaving Kim hardened, determined. Clea was Flow's girl and he was going to find a way to accept it.

Still, he couldn't bring himself to ask Flow how it was going and Flow didn't offer any information. They watched TV, smoked cigarettes, played computer games and threw things into the bin from various corners of the room.

The journalist who picked up the story of the food fight used the Doria Road flat as a backdrop, which effectively showcased their design work. Clea's profile looked impressive, with her Paris stint and professional photos, online for all to see.

Diary dear diary,

I am now scared out of my wits. I simply do not understand Hugo's obsession. He hasn't touched me since Clea left, that I am glad about, my skin has started to physically crawl whenever he is near me. I am not sleeping. He gets up and paces even more often at night, and he goes to Clea's room, muttering and ranting.

Gold

It wasn't long before Clea got an audition for a West End show, bagging a supporting role, plus Kim and Flow got a commission to do up a boutique hotel near Bermondsey Street – all was steaming ahead.

They had dismantled their crop of grass from the roof of the flats, sad to let go of their first successful business venture but realising it was time.

They were soon to move out of Doria Road, having rented a flat near Bermondsey Street. They had the work to bankroll it, now, instead of pursuing their garage idea.

Kim had finally got through to the principal on the phone after lots of failed attempts. She had been aloof, saying health issues and the politics of him being an ex-student had stopped her taking things further, but he had managed to persuade her to come and talk to him at the flat. He said how much it would mean to him for her to see what he had been working on whilst being at her college.

Flow had gone off to Spain for a holiday with his family so unusually, Kim had the place to himself.

'Wow,' said Kim when he opened the door to her. She was so beautiful, he thought, and she smiled at his appreciation, despite herself.

'So,' she said. 'This is what you were working on all that time, huh?' She gestured at the impressive surroundings, taking a turn around every room.

'Yep,' said Kim, opening a cupboard with various bottles inside of it. 'Whisky?'

The Frog Theory

'Try tea,' said the principal. 'I'm driving.' Kim flicked the kettle on.

'Tea,' he said, lining up the mug and the teabag. 'Just Tetleys, hope that's okay? Haven't got any of that la-di-da shit.'

'Tetleys fine,' said the principal, sitting on one of the sofas.

There was silence as they waited for the kettle. 'Goddamn it,' she said. 'Just give me a whisky. I lied about driving here.'

Kim prepared the drinks without comment and sat next to her. 'Can we just go to bed?' she suggested, feeling the Devil whirl her away in his incredibly fast car.

It was Clea's first night on stage. All went well, only a couple of little mistakes that nobody noticed, and the cast hit the town afterwards to celebrate, still in costume.

Clea's was a short, gold, figure-hugging dress. Gold-flecked hair, dramatic gold make-up and impossibly high (gold) shoes – completed the look. She didn't usually drink much but she sure made up for it tonight, keeping pace with her contemporaries, who were much more accustomed.

When one of them offered her a bit more than a drink, she found herself snorting something white off a wrap. This was out of character for her, but she had been seriously spooked. She could have sworn she saw Hugo when she'd come out of the stage door; in fact, she was more or less certain.

But the powder had made the feeling of terror so much worse. She was totally overwhelmed, out of it, insecure. It was just her, alone in the world, same as always.

All she could think was that she had to find Kim because he was the answer.

'Doria Road,' she whispered to herself as she searched for a taxi, clutching her purse-full of cash.

Kim was surprised to hear the bell ring. He thought Flow had come back early from Spain for some reason and had lost his keys, so he imagined for a moment he was dreaming when he saw Clea standing there like a pillar of gold.

'I need you,' she said, clearly the worse for wear and swaying slightly.

'Flow's in Spain,' he answered.

'Flow?' she said, confused. That wasn't who she wanted to see at all. 'It's *you* I came to see…to sort out the frog,' she explained, holding the doorframe to steady herself as the principal came to the door to see what was going on. She was fully dressed, ready to flee a difficult situation if necessary.

'Everything okay?' she said to both of them.

'The frog theory,' said Kim, twigging. 'Clea's in hot water.'

'I just finished the first night of the show…Tequila…think I might be sick so…' she left the sentence hanging.

'Oh, for fuck's sake,' said Kim, ushering her down the hall towards the bathroom.

Clea slammed the bathroom door.

'Who's *that?*' asked the principal, eyebrow raised.

'Flow's girlfriend,' said Kim.

'Wow,' said the principal as they returned to the sitting room, standing around waiting. 'The one from the food fight, of course,' she surmised.

Presently, Clea swayed unsteadily towards them.

'I wasn't sick after all,' she announced slurringly, approaching the principal.

She stared at her in a way that the principal found most unnerving.

'What are you looking at? Why are you looking at me there?' she asked.

Clea's eyes had settled on a patch on the principal's chest, the patch where a doctor had taken X-rays following persistent pain in that area. He'd sent her for a biopsy which now sat in a petri dish in a lab somewhere. Just a small pin-prick where the needle went in, nothing Kim would have noticed, or anyone else for that matter, yet this girl stared like she knew, through the top she was wearing.

The Frog Theory

'You've got a secret you don't like.'

'Leave her,' Kim intervened protectively.

'No,' said the principal. 'Let her carry on.'

'Near your heart, I can see it,' said Clea. She held her hands toward it and the principal felt a great warmth in the place where the pain came and went. It felt as if hot light particles were dispersing the mass she held there. Clea held her hands close and shut her eyes for a good few minutes.

'What's happening?' said Kim, eventually.

'I told you, she's got a secret...it's like she doesn't want it and she doesn't know how to get it out.'

'What secret?' said Kim.

'Shut up,' said the principal, her heart pumping frantically. Kim backed towards the kitchen area, his hands up in surrender.

'I made it stop hurting,' said Clea.

They locked eyes and the principal felt full of light.

'Can you see what my secret is?' she asked.

'No,' said Clea. 'I just saw it in my mind's eye and got a sense of your pain...like you're getting a sense of mine now – although you can't quite place it.' She began to stagger.

'What is it?' said Kim, striding back into their space. 'What's the matter?'

'I'm so dizzy,' said Clea with a half-hearted laugh, her eyes glittering.

'Did you take anything?' he said, shaking her urgently, looking into her eyes.

'Some white powder,' she said. 'I don't know what it was,' she added, before passing out.

The principal was well-versed in such situations, she even carried a pot of charcoal powder in her handbag. Clea soon came around, after which, she took her to the bathroom. She made her throw up and got her to drink a mixture of charcoal and water to soak up the toxins. She then put her in Flow's bed to sleep, returning to the main living area.

The weird thing was that any physical pain the principal had been suffering had stopped completely, it was peculiar.

'What was all that stuff about a secret?' asked Kim.

'She knew,' said the principal. 'She said my secret was killing me.'

'She said it was *hurting* you, actually,' corrected Kim. 'I *was* there, you know.'

'But you don't understand,' said the principal. 'She was right. I had a lump exactly where she did that thing and I *do* have a secret.' She sank into the sofa, holding her hand over her heart. 'A truly terrible secret that clearly doesn't want to be a secret anymore…be a darling, fix me another whisky?' She nodded towards the bottle, still on the kitchen counter top. 'And let's see what you think of me when you've heard *this* sorry little tale.'

She described how she had caught her sister in bed with Mike and for the first time ever, told an outside party what had happened afterwards.

'I told my sister to get dressed and go home and she did, without looking at me or saying a word. Then Mike and I had the almightiest row, as you would expect but…he wasn't even slightly repentant.

'He hated our life together, it turned out…he was bored. Suffocated – didn't love the children, didn't love me. It was so unbelievably hurtful.

'I realise now – dealing with personality disorders at the college – that he is probably a narcissist, in a medical sense… but it doesn't excuse what I did.

'I said if you hate your life so much I'll buy you a plane ticket and give you some money, tell everyone you're dead and you can go back to your beloved Australia. Start again – erase us.

'He was always going on about how terrible England was, he said even the tap water *tasted like snot*.' He could be so disgusting and so negative.

'But I never thought for a minute he would really agree.

'Turns out he thought it was a fantastic idea – a total 'get out

The Frog Theory

of jail free' card so...I bought his ticket and said he had gone home for a family emergency, that his mum had suffered a blip in her health.

'I thought he would come to his senses but he kept going along with the plan...pushing it forwards...I found I couldn't backtrack.

'We got a divorce on-line...I didn't even know such a thing existed...no courts, no solicitor's fees...I gave him thirty thousand pounds, which is all the money I could muster, without Ma finding out. Thirty – thousand – pounds...in exchange for *us*, his family.' She paused to take some whisky, clutching the glass like a crystal ball. 'Mike didn't have anyone, really,' she continued. 'His mum was already in a home, mad as a box of frogs...'

What was it with bloody frog metaphors, thought Kim?

'Father died when he was young...and he has a brother out there who doesn't even talk to him.

'And perhaps this is the worst bit.

'I got an urn and filled it with cat litter, told everyone here that he had drowned whilst surfing...and that we had got his ashes. We had a family ceremony on the top of a cliff and... Mike was gone.'

'Kitty litter!' snorted Kim, unable to keep a straight face. 'Sorry but I honestly thought you were going to tell me that you had *murdered* him and I've got to say...I'm kinda relieved you didn't.'

'*Relieved?*' said the principal incongruously. She was confused and full of self-loathing as her secret sprawled territorially around the room. Saying it out loud was one thing but she had to work out what to do with the creature, now that it was out.

'I was imagining the headlines – disgruntled mother of two buries husband under patio after finding him in bed with...' The principal smiled a little. 'Yes, I'm relieved. I think what you did is probably a crime of some sort in the eyes of the law but...murdering him would have been way worse, obviously...

and I think we all do things that disgust or disappoint ourselves at some point.'

'Have you?' she asked.

'Yeah,' he said, not offering any more information, although she waited. He contemplated the thing that haunted him.

The bike pedal incident, when he was seven. He would never share the story with anyone. Only two people knew what that was really about – himself and the man who had done it.

Kim had been playing with Flow and Pat outside on the estate after school and they had needed a magnifying glass to see whether they could direct the sun's rays through it and set fire to some old twigs. (They had tried using Pat's glasses to no avail.)

Kim remembered the magnifying glass they had at home and, despite *express* instructions to stay out of the flat, had decided that he would gallantly go in and get it.

Quietly he had crept to the lounge, finding the glass exactly where he remembered, next to the landline. His mum used it often, always saying she should get her eyes tested but never getting around to it.

He was home and dry with the object of desire, almost out of the flat, when unusual noises coming from the bedroom had halted him.

Curious, he had crept towards the noise, a man grunting – not quite in pain but something else. The bedroom door was ajar, plenty of room for a small boy to peep inside. From his viewpoint he could see the end of his mum's bed, over which she hung, face down, hair touching the floor and, on top of her, a large man moving rhythmically.

As if he felt Kim's stare he had looked up – discovering his young voyeur. The man had maintained eye contact until he was done.

Kim then fled before his mum could tell him off for coming into the flat, but he wasn't fast enough. The man was upon him, smashing his head on the pedal of a bicycle leaning against the wall in the hallway.

The Frog Theory

The memory had remained vivid but the feelings that went with it had altered significantly.

Initially, he had seen something that he didn't understand but it had not been unpleasant, simply a new experience – he was fine with that.

He believed the man had punished him because he had gone into the flat when he had been told *expressly* by his mother that he wasn't allowed. He was fine with that.

As he got older he realised he had seen his mum buggered by a client – *not* fine with that. The client hadn't stopped when he saw him because it had heightened his pleasure – *not* fine with that. Kim himself had stayed and watched rather than walking away – *not* fine with that. The client had knocked him out on the bike pedal – *not* fine with that. His mum was a prostitute – *not* fine with that.

He wished that he had been repelled and had stopped looking. But he had watched right through to the end. He had been a naïve little boy, true to a base sense of nature that had intrigued him at the time, and nothing could change it.

The guy had knocked Kim out, because the incident had made him hate himself. He might like going to a prostitute, but in front of a small boy? No. He'd lashed out physically, frantically calling upon his personal spin doctor to make a story he could live with; *it was the boy's fault, not his own.*

And therein lay the epiphany of the lesson – people disappointed themselves. They harboured personality traits, good and bad, forever dormant or destined to be conjured by some unexpected situation.

Kim had resolved to do his best not to disappoint himself. His scar was a constant reminder of that. But now that the list of things he wasn't fine about had finally stopped getting longer, he realised he should put it to rest, otherwise a few years later, he might find himself getting all tangled up.

'Thinking of it now for the first time in how long…so what? It was some kind of crazy experience, is all,' he said. 'It taught me...that people disappoint themselves...and it's actually made me think before I do shit.' He subconsciously touched his scar, humbled. 'You wish you had done something different but you did what you did...at the time...and going back to you, it probably saved your kids from a right old handful of a man.'

'I never looked at it like that...they were only little of course...both under five, and Mike was hardly home, working on night shoots, earning a lot of money, though you wouldn't know it because he spent *everything*.' She changed tack. 'Men never asked me out, girls were jealous of me, I was so unhappy I even thought about suicide. The modelling was meant to be fun, lighten me up. Then Mike...threw himself at me like I was the most incredible thing he'd ever seen and I was flattered, appreciated, *wanted*. My sister always craved whatever I had, she was horribly jealous. Sleeping with my husband was in a whole new league, though...I never told my mother what she did and neither did she. It was satisfying telling Sophie he was dead, that her *lover* had been taken away.' She spat the word lover, surprising herself. She looked appalled.

They continued to talk it through and her thoughts came timidly forward, monsters in the dark. Mistakes.

They checked on Clea. She had flung the covers off and was sprawled across the bed in the large T-shirt the principal had put her in.

'She's very beautiful,' said the principal.

'You think so?' said Kim. 'I could never quite tell when we first met.' He was unaware of how fondly he was looking at Clea and of how quizzically the principal was looking at him.

'Goodbye, gorgeous girl,' she said, kissing Clea gently on the cheek. 'And thank you,' she whispered, putting her hand on her own chest where it was still warm with her light.

'Come,' she said to Kim. 'Help me find a taxi.'

She linked his arm as they walked towards the New King's Road together. They went at a leisurely pace along the pretty street

The Frog Theory

filled with terraced houses. The cherry trees were blossoming and even in the darkness the petals glowed pink in the soft light of the street lamps.

'She's in love with you, you know?'

'She's in love with Flow,' said Kim, firmly.

They continued in silence until they reached the main street and hailed a taxi. 'I can come back to yours?' offered Kim.

'I think you should be there when she wakes up,' replied the principal, studying his face. He wanted to kiss her but all emotional doorways seemed locked.

'This is goodbye for you, isn't it?' he said.

When she didn't answer he carried on. 'You've done more for me—'

'And you for me,' she interrupted, getting into the taxi. 'We'll get coffee next week!' she called, as she closed the door. But he knew it was her way of making goodbye easier and that whatever they had done for each other was just that – done.

One-to-one

Kim returned to Doria Road and slumped on one of the sofas in the dark. He watched the shadows play around the room cast by the lights from the gardens of a busy London district that was his birthplace, Fulham, and realised that he was well and truly ready to leave.

He wasn't sure how much time passed, only that he woke up cold with a start and took a few moments to piece everything together. He went to check on Clea, finding her still sleeping peacefully in Flow's bed.

Shivering, he decided to take a hot shower. The sun was nearly up and he wasn't going to go back to sleep now. The hot water restored him and afterwards he returned to his bedroom to find some clothes, a towel wrapped around his waist.

'What happened?' said Clea sleepily, wandering into his room.

'Oh, nothing much,' said Kim, pulling on underwear, jeans, shirt. Clea was too busy clutching her head to even notice his brief moment of nakedness. 'You just turned up at one in the morning, or whatever it was, looking like a pillar of gold, said you thought you were going to be sick, then did some sort of voodoo healing thing on my guest before passing out on the floor, but apart from that...'

'What?' said Clea. 'What healing thing? Doesn't sound like me.'

'Well, maybe a tea or coffee will help refresh your memory – how's your head?'

'Fuzzy...and look at me,' said Clea, surveying the smudged stage make-up in his bedroom mirror. 'Actually, don't look at me, what a mess,' she said, scrubbing at her face with a tissue. The slick layer over her skin felt disgusting and she longed to wash it off properly; a large amount of it had transferred onto Flow's pillow slip – *embarrassing*.

She began to recall the night's events. 'I remember drinking too much,' she said, following him down the hall.

'Uhhhh-ha,' said Kim, flicking the kettle on.

'Then I remember being totally out of it and freaked and the only thing...' she stopped and looked at him, blushing.

'The only thing?' he prompted her, locking eyes.

'The only thing I could think, was that I had to get to you,' she finished, looking right back without flinching or blushing, now.

It was Kim's turn to feel uncomfortable.

'Errrrr, tea or coffee?' he asked in the end.

'Why didn't you kiss me that night in the park, Kim?' she asked boldly.

'Clea, I don't feel very comfortable with this, what with Flow and you the way it is, and Flow being my best mate, it's not ethical, you know what I mean?'

'There is no Flow and me, Kim, there never was.' She tugged at the T-shirt, realising that it only just covered her bottom. 'Coffee, please – and can I have a quick shower?' She threw the tissue into one of the holes in the bin area, it was brilliantly satisfying.

The Frog Theory

'No – I mean of course, have a shower. No Flow and you, is what I meant, what do you mean?'

'I mean we have never even kissed, we're just friends. Always have been just friends.'

'What about that night you stayed? After the food fight?'

'I slept on the sofa, Flow slept in his bed.' She took the coffee gratefully and sipped. 'It's like he knew I liked you,' she said openly. She was being very brave, maybe she was still drunk or high or both. 'Was that your girlfriend here last night?' she said, forgetting the shower for the moment, curling her long legs under her on the sofa, cupping the warm mug with her hands. 'She's seriously beautiful.'

Kim sat next to her, a little smile playing on his face.

'No you and Flow?' he said.

'No – me – and – Flow,' she levelled, a smile playing on her face too as she enjoyed unselfconsciously looking at him for once, her tummy flipping pleasantly.

'No you and Flow,' he said, while the information sank in. 'And you like me.'

'That's what I said.'

'And he's okay about that?'

'You'd know that better than me,' said Clea, thinking how happy Kim was looking. 'Was it bothering you?'

'Yeah,' said Kim. 'It was bothering me.'

'Does that mean you like me, too?' said Clea.

'What do you think?' said Kim.

Clea wanted to ask him again whether that had been his girlfriend but her boldness had gone.

'I think I've been very honest with you,' she answered.

'That wasn't my girlfriend,' said Kim, as if he had read her mind. 'She came to tell me…well, she came to say goodbye.'

Saying it broke their eye contact and also broke the spell.

'Okay,' she said, conscious of the change in atmosphere. She made a mental note to stick the pillow-slip in a pile of dirty washing she had noticed, while they took a few beats to re-group. 'I do remember the healing thing,' she said thoughtfully.

'But I've never done it before, it must have been something to do with being off my head, on another wavelength, whatever it was. I seriously have no idea but it seemed to just happen. I felt like I could see her problem and grab it – she had a secret – I don't know what it was but it was hurting her, literally. Unless I imagined it all.'

'That's what you kept saying, that she had a secret you could see. Anyway, maybe you were right, maybe she did have a secret and maybe you helped.' He looked at her again, she looked back and the bubble of their original relationship began to re-form and surround them. 'You should get that shower.'

He got up, nervous that he might just grab her if he stayed too close. 'Whatever you need's in there, towels...all that,' he said, touching his scar.

He wanted to talk to Flow. He had to know it was going to be okay with him and if it wasn't, this was going nowhere. He couldn't risk their friendship. He would be nothing without it.

Secret's out

In the same way that a song or a fragrance could transport a person to somewhere lost and unobtainable, Kim and Clea had connected the principal back to a time and a situation, that all the good deeds in the present had failed to fix.

Safely in her house, she cried like never before. For everything. For hours. She could have kept the tears at bay so easily; just a crook of her finger would have had Kim in the taxi with her, willingly giving away yet more of his young energy to warm herself against.

But she had already taken too much, buckling under the pressure of being human, and now that she could finally see the wreckage, she could pick her way through.

The doctor closed the door and asked her to sit down. The biopsy had showed that the lump was not dangerous or malignant, but he recommended surgery to remove it.

'About that.'

She explained that the lump seemed to have disappeared.

'That's odd,' said the doctor. He had a good feel around and agreed that there was nothing. 'Well maybe it was just a cyst, they do come and go...and maybe the biopsy encouraged the body to send white cells to the area...' he explained, but he looked slightly perplexed. They agreed that she would come back if there was any problem but for now, she could go.

Contact with Mike had been scarce but consistent. He would sometimes ask her for money and without fail, she would put whatever he suggested into his account, for fear that he would rock the boat if she did not. As soon as she got back from the doctor's, she got in touch with him and told him she was going to tell the children the truth. He was accepting, and she hoped it was because he felt as bad as she, rather than the need to top up his bank balance.

Clea's influence had done more than *physically* alter the blockage. It had emotionally altered it too, by reminding her of how young she had been – a similar age to them, in fact. Now that she was more experienced, she could re-visit the situation with fresh eyes.

There was no way to predict how her children would react, they may never want to speak to her again, but at least she could think it through as optimistically as possible.

Hopefully, they would want to see Mike, and it was sensible for them to go to Australia, rather than for him to walk back into the house like a ghost.

Flow

Flow had really enjoyed some time out with his family during their holiday in Spain. It was so easy to be with them all – even his brother had been good company. They went out a lot, lunching in nice restaurants by the beach or staying in the villa, lounging around the pool.

And his mum had done most of the cooking when they stayed in – often with his nan alongside her, though he had insisted on doing dinner one evening, to show off his new skill. He wished he could have bottled their looks of amazement.

His mum had complimented him on the way he had grown up lately; said she was proud. It was a moment for him. Leaving home had helped him break away from the accepted view of himself, the *carefree joker*.

Apparently, Jackie was with Ryan, now – pregnant but not yet married. It was like watching a show of what his life could have turned into and he felt immeasurably relieved that he had escaped. A huge jug of sangria found its way down him after the news, followed by a refreshing slumber by the pool.

Now he was back, he was happy to be in a pub with Kim, the chatter around him buzzing and friendly. *This* was the life he wanted.

Nobody apart from Kim knew his past, here, everything was fresh. He was free from Jackie's leash and could mash potatoes without people sniggering that he had once got it so wrong.

'I have to ask you…where are you at with Clea, Flow? I thought you liked her?'

Flow stared into his pint, slightly less happy all of a sudden – embarrassed, in fact. He hadn't mentioned to Kim that nothing romantic had ever transpired.

'Why? What are you asking me for?'

'Just…curious,' said Kim, bottling it.

They gave each other one of those sideways glances they knew so well and went silently back to their pints.

'Well, you don't slam a strawberry gateau in someone's face unless you're really fucking angry,' said Flow as last. 'And I figured she must really like *you* to do that, like most girls – story of my life,' he added enviously with another sideways glance and a raised eyebrow, before returning once again to his pint.

They glugged in unpeaceful silence, surveying the pub.

'So…has anything happened with you and her that I should know about?' said Flow eventually.

'No. I promise, no.'

'But you want it to, right?'

The Frog Theory

'No! Not if it's going to fuck us up.'

'But you like her?' he pushed.

'Yeah, I like her.'

'Like her just want to have a good time with her like her, or *like* her like her?'

'*Like* her, Flow, but not enough to fuck us up. I just wanted to sound you out, that's all. No big deal. I can take it or leave it and I'm going to leave it. I don't know why I even brought it up. It's nothing.'

'Huh!' snorted Flow, sarcastically.

'And just what is that supposed to mean?'

'It means "huh", Kim, it just means "huh", okay?'

'No, it's not okay, Flow. I'm not falling out with you over a girl again, never, you hear? You're family to me. Us not talking was the worst time of my life and fuck knows I've had a lot of worst times. Forget I said anything, just don't give me shit, okay?'

'Okay,' said Flow. 'Fuck. All I said was huh,' he mumbled into his pint.

'It's the *way* you said huh, Flow. Don't fuck with me on this.'

'Okay, I huh...earrrd you,' he said, with a smile in his voice.

'You think you're so funny, don't you? Just remember all the dirt I've got on you. What would your mum say if she knew you were the one who taught the parrot to shout "fuck you, you fucking fuck"? *Huh?*'

'She grounded my brother for a week.'

'I know,' said Kim. 'You want me to carry on?'

Slowly over the evening the synergy returned to their friendship. Kim had forgotten Clea once before, he would forget her again.

Once Clea had further slept off her over-indulgences, she replayed events and cringed. How could she have been so forward with Kim? What had she been thinking? Plus, taking a strange white powder – absolute madness, she had worked too hard to put everything at risk like that.

She needed to get a serious grip of herself if she wanted her career to go anywhere. Her performance hadn't been as good after God knows what rubbish she had put into her body; she had been so thirsty, downing pints and pints of water for four days after that.

Her Achilles heel, her weakness for Kim, threatened to make a fool of her – how did her feelings for him manage to overshadow everything else that was so much more important in her life?

Every time she saw him she lost control, every time. Not only that, during this latest episode she had made a complete freak of herself with the healing thing. She had no idea how that had happened but it had spooked her. She resolved to put an end to it with a text.

> I'm so sorry for coming to you in that state,
> it won't happen again. Thank you for your help. Cxx

It wasn't long before she got a message back from Kim.

> Probably best. Good luck with the show. K

No kiss at the end. He wasn't interested. 'Probably best' – *good*. But her stomach lurched and the old ache threatened. She took his beer bottle letter out of her purse where she had sentimentally tucked it and made to tear it up but she couldn't quite bring herself to do it. Instead, she shoved it between a couple of books and went to have a hot shower before it was time to leave for the theatre.

She stepped outside with her usual trepidation and looked around nervously for Hugo but how odd; the vibe had gone. Even when she *tried* to call the fearful feeling to mind, it simply was not there – no hateful radio transmission anymore.

She stood still for a moment, contemplating the date. It was her mother's birthday. Strange, that they were no longer in touch. She walked down the road with a new sense of confusion, almost like she was missing a hole in the head, which had been replaced by the feeling that she might be just a little bit crazy.

Coming clean

The principal sat her children around the kitchen table and told them she had something very upsetting to admit. She explained things as best and as honestly as she could, unsure of what their reactions might be. She detailed the characteristics of a narcissist, and her suspicion that Mike might be one, encouraging them to accept that there might be a medical aspect to his behaviour, hopefully helping them to feel less jilted.

'Aunt Sophie did that, Mum?' her daughter asked in amazement. 'It certainly makes sense of the weird atmosphere whenever we see her at Granny's…and why she never comes to the house, although she lives so close. But she's not a narcissist, so…you can't really get *her* off the hook, can you?'

'Warped! And sick…you're way better looking than Aunt Sophie, Mum. I mean…' He halted his stream of consciousness, aware of how shallow he sounded. 'I know there's more than looks but…messed up…that you told us he was dead. Though I take on board the narcissist element…I think…and it was Dad who kind of drove this thing, really, I also think…rather than you.'

'Well,' said the principal, 'now things are out in the open we should go and see him, where he lives in Australia, so that we can both apologise to you and work out…' she stopped.

'Work out what?' said her daughter.

'Well, what we do next…as a…' she faltered again. 'Family,' she finished uneasily. 'How do you feel?'

'Shocked, relieved…it explains how weird you've been, I thought it was because of his death…but it was because of his *fake* death. I feel like I hate him for doing that…for sleeping with Aunt Sophie and then for agreeing he would leave… and encouraging you to tell us he was dead…shit, Mum, you married a crazy man!'

'Agree,' said her son.

'I don't know if I even want to see him, I cried so much imagining this perfect father I should have in my life...how he would have given me away...all sorts of silly dreams...Mum, what about Granny? She'll be so upset, I'm not sure what or how...'

'One step at a time, Emily.' The principal slowed her down. 'I think we should book tickets and visit him, while we can... before we go any further thinking about it...and spend some time in Australia, get Mike's input...see what he's like, we don't even know him.' She opened a window on her laptop for them to see, scrolling through some nice hotels. 'None of us have been there, it will move things forward and help us re-order our emotions...give us some time away together, removed from our everyday lives.'

'I'm in shock, Mum,' said Emily. 'I feel like I should hate you or something...but I don't, I definitely feel relieved that it's out in the open.'

'Me too,' said her brother.

They flew to Australia a couple of days later but they didn't want to stay with Mike after all that had happened. It was their mother who had stuck around and loved them, not him. He didn't offer, anyway, so the principal chose a nice hotel, with a family room, in order to spoil them.

She felt it was the least she could do and they were surprisingly loving. They lay on the big bed watching movies together, and ordered room service. They arranged to meet Mike the following morning. The principal was very tearful. She had held back tears for so long that they seemed to be endlessly down-loading the backlog.

Resurrected

They sat in a booth in a diner, the chosen spot to meet, waiting for Mike to come back from the dead.

When he walked in they all took in his slightly bedraggled

The Frog Theory

appearance. He was still a good-looking man but there was something pathetic and browbeaten in his demeanour and his hair was way too long.

He slid into the booth, into their lives, and looked at them curiously.

'So,' said the principal. 'How have you been?'

'Okay,' he answered. 'Been surfing, the waves are awesome! You surf?' he asked his son.

Had he always had such a pronounced Australian drawl? thought the principal.

'Cut the small talk,' said her son with a level stare. 'I want to know why you slept with Aunt Sophie.'

'Huh?' said Mike. 'Who told you that?'

'I told them, Mike, how else was I going to explain why we lied?'

'Well thanks a bunch,' he said, crossing his arms in a childish sulk.

'Well?' pushed his son.

'She wanted it, I gave it to her,' he explained simply, shrugging his shoulders.

'For how long?' cut in the principal, unable to stop herself, ready to know.

'What does it matter now? It's all in the past,' said Mike.

'It matters to me,' snapped the principal, her eyes stinging with some sort of emotion she couldn't yet identify.

'And me,' said their daughter, almost too quietly to hear.

'From the beginning, since you ask,' said Mike. 'It was when we were dating and she would always give me the come-on. You never noticed and we only got it together a couple of times but she would want more – pissed me off! I tried to tell her I wasn't interested – like that day you caught us, such a pisser. It was her bloody fault, stalking me, literally, as soon as she knew you were away at your mum's, calling, texting. And I get the fucking blame, me? Hey!' he called to the waitress. 'Can I get a drink over here? Iced coffee? The waffles are awesome,' he said to the table in general to find three pairs of eyes staring incredulously at him. 'What?' he asked. 'What did I do?'

'Do you feel the least bit bad about what you did?' asked the principal calmly.

'What *she* did!' he countered. 'I told you it wasn't my fault. I tried to tell you at the time but you wouldn't listen – just talked me into the stupid *dead* thing. Can't believe I went along with it, by the way. I'm not taking the rap for this, get *her* here to take the blame, get Sophie.' He crossed his arms again. 'Anyway, it was ages ago and the main thing is we're together now, right? You're over whatever weird breakdown thing you had and we should like…get some waffles, check out the surf…move on.' He did a wave movement with his hand to emphasise his point.

They stared at him in stunned silence.

'You kids are looking at me like that but you should give me a fucking break, start blaming your weirdo mother, not me, it was her idea.' He glared at them all.

'Okay, studying medicine, as I do,' began their daughter. 'I'm pretty sure that what Mum experienced back then was a psychotic break, triggered by a traumatic event – such as *finding your narcissistic husband in bed with your sister*!' She glared back at him.

The waitress put a coffee down in front of Mike.

'Can I get some waffles?'

'Sure,' said the waitress, pad at the ready. 'Anyone want anything else?'

'Emmmmmmm…I don't know, maybe I should have the bacon and eggs – Mum? What you gonna go for?'

'I'm sticking with coffee just…*choose*,' she said impatiently to her son.

'Incredible. That you could blame Mum,' continued their daughter. 'You left us, walked away…from *your* mistake, blaming Aunt Sophie – you're pathetic. Like you couldn't say no and now you're saying that Mum was weird and Mum was

The Frog Theory

mad, that she *made* you lie as if you had no choice in the matter? You're a fucking dick.'

'Hey!' said Mike, standing up, but not entirely straight because of the angle of the booth and the table. 'Like I need this shit.'

'It's all my fault,' said the principal, the cool she managed to keep for so many years crumbling around her, yet again. 'I don't deserve to be a mother. I've failed you so badly, I've let you down, I can't stand it!' Her son put a protective arm around her.

'Don't you dare blame yourself, Mum,' said her daughter. 'She did everything for us, *Dad* – sent us to the best schools, bought us nice clothes...living with that guilt all the time – every day. If you want to walk out now, do it. How dare you criticise, she didn't say a single bad thing about you, only what you had done, without judgement.'

'I can't even call you *Dad*. I'll punch you right here, right now, if you say another word against her, so you'd better think really hard about what you say next.'

There were a few beats whist Mike looked from one to the other.

'I'm outnumbered,' he said. 'You're all against me, blaming me, I never stood a chance.' And with that he slid out of the booth. 'I'm seriously out of here,' he called, as he pushed the door open and left.

'Mum, they're both tossers,' said her son. 'Him *and* your stupid sister – wipe your eyes, have some breakfast.'

'I'd say you were spot on with your narcissist theory,' agreed her daughter. 'He'll pick himself right up and move on without any discomfort what-so-ever...while we are in pieces, and haven't we wasted enough time? *You're* my father...and my mother...at least he gave us life...I can honestly say I am grateful for *that*.'

How did her children get so wise?

Emily looked at the waffles going cold. 'I kind of need to stop thinking about it for a while...it's the shock...it's too much to take in.' She looked up. 'Let's enjoy our breakfast and some time with *you* away from that *fucking college!*' She crammed her mouth full.

The principal ignored the swearing, she had given up on that long ago.

'I can't stop looking at you both, now that I don't have to carry that awful secret,' she said, her eyes filling with tears yet again. 'You're so beautiful…you're my babies, and I'm so very…very sorry.'

She surveyed their young, fresh faces, leaning over to stroke their hair.

'Mum,' her son said. 'You're *embarrassing* me now.' Emily laughed.

'You embarrass yourself *most* of the time, quit stressing!'

The secret had disintegrated. Time and retrospect may twist and change their feelings, but she would cross those bridges if and *when* she came to them. 'Now' was precious, *now* was where they were, and it was enough.

The kiss

The show was demanding, six nights a week, then a four-day break once every six weeks, which didn't give Clea much time to socialise. However, she had managed to go on some dates with an attractive guy, and to get intimate. The world had definitely – not – moved, but at least she had experienced a bit of romance, and it had been a useful comparison to the out of control feelings she had experienced with Kim.

She was still in touch with Flow and considered him to be one of her best friends, though they did not physically see each other, they communicated mostly by text and the occasional phone call.

She had settled into a flat-share with Melissa and was still loving their friendship, feeling more at home than she had ever felt in her life. Melissa also had work, in a small play at The Old Vic. Charlie and his daughter had come to see it with Clea, during her time off. His daughter was so much like Charlie, it was uncanny; Clea suspected she might be gay and had it confirmed when she openly discussed her girlfriend over dinner.

Flow and Kim were doing nicely in their rented flat. Life at home went on pretty much as it had in Doria Road, except they were working for money as well as job satisfaction, now. The town house in Bermondsey Square was rapidly becoming a boutique hotel, as commissioned. The bedrooms had wet-rooms installed, hidden by floor-to-ceiling cupboards that were on roller blades. Roll one sideways and *ta daaaa!* There was your bathroom, with different artwork in each – Flow's 'tag'. They had two more projects queuing.

Social life around the area was spectacular – there seemed to be no division of class, and a lot of creative people around with ideas in common. Plus, with Borough Market just down the road, you could pick up great cuts of meat and fish for very little, if you knew which days to go on.

But Flow felt increasingly conflicted. He had a nag that he had halted something special between Kim and Clea, although there was no shortage of girls for them, he felt guilty.

When he explored his feelings further, he reflected that Kim and Clea had a lot in common that wasn't immediately obvious. They were both only children, for a start, with violent backgrounds. And they both had estranged fathers – and when they were in the same room you could just tell there was something there, although he had tried his best to deny it.

Yes, he liked Clea. She had been the only ray of hope when things had been falling apart with Jackie and that talisman was hard to let go of, even now. *He* had been the one to look after her when she had split her lip – shit, he'd even spray-painted a Porsche in her honour, so he felt protective and very much like she was his discovery.

It was definitely a friendship that was never going to be a romance, though. They were in touch, *as friends*, and he had promised to go to her show, but the problem was that he didn't know how to approach it with Kim, and he didn't want to go to her show behind his back.

They hadn't spoken about Clea since their near-spat over it in the pub and true to his word, Kim had not been in touch with her at all, which made him feel like a spoilt brat.

Knowing Kim, the way he did, he figured springing it on him would be best, before he had time to think about it, so he contacted Clea, sorted out getting together – and did exactly that.

'I asked Clea out for a drink.' He dropped casually into conversation.

'Oh?' said Kim, immediately on high alert, as Flow had expected – he needed to play this right.

The Frog Theory

'We're going to pick her up at her place, eight o'clock,' he said, like it was nothing.

'What do you mean, *we*,' said Kim. 'And are you talking about tonight?'

'Yeah,' said Flow. 'She's performing so much of the time, it was a spontaneous kind of a thing...'

'That you *spontaneously* involved me in?' finished Kim.

'Yeah,' said Flow, as they exchanged one of their looks. 'I like one of the waitresses in Bar East and I thought we should all go there...she's working tonight.'

'So now you're pairing me up with Clea? Is that it?' said Kim, pissed off. 'Because suddenly that's okay with you?'

'Yeah,' said Flow. 'Is there a problem?' Kim considered. He wanted to see Clea again.

'I guess...not.' He finished, surprised at himself. 'Thanks.' He softened.

They rang the intercom at Clea's apartment block. It was old-fashioned of them to go and call for her that way, rather than simply meeting her at the bar, but she had offered to show them around the flat. Kim recalled her flying out of the house in Alderville Road like a nervous wild thing, slamming the door behind her, all that time ago, when she had been under Hugo's thumb.

'Hi Kim,' she said, giving nothing away. He felt a stab of heartache and touched his scar to ground himself. 'So, this is it,' she said, showing them around the flat, moving so gracefully that both of them admired her.

'And this is my room.'

She had finished the tour.

'Nice,' said Flow, opening and closing a wardrobe, as Kim checked out the bookshelf. *The Book Thief*. He'd read that and it was incredible. 'Where's the loo?' asked Flow.

Kim continued to scour the books for something to do whilst they waited for Flow, and his eye fell upon a piece of paper that had his writing on it.

Clea had been following his gaze and hers rested, along with his, on the beer bottle letter she had stuck between the books.

'Don't touch that!' she shouted, more loudly than she had intended.

'You climbed your mum's house and got it, didn't you?' said Kim, not fooled for a second.

'So what if I did?' said Clea.

It calmed his anxiety to have the upper hand once more and he tried to conceal a smile.

'It's not funny,' said Clea, her emotions raw around him already.

'Look...could we just have some sort of a truce?' asked Kim. 'If you and Flow are going to be friends then...*we* need to be friends...okay?'

The problem was that she wasn't sure she could cope with *friends* when it came to Kim, and now that he had seen the letter she'd been sentimental enough to keep, it was *her* personal feelings all over the table yet again.

His presence always connected her to a damaged part of herself, inert behind a little door, until he inexplicably flicked it open with such ease. She should never have agreed to see him again, never.

'Clea?' he said, seeing her downcast expression.

'We fit to go for that drink, then?' said Flow.

'Can you give us a second?' asked Kim.

'Sure.'

He left the room and as soon as the door clicked shut, Kim was somehow close, kissing her – making up for everything. She was enveloped, her whole body responding in a way she had never experienced before. She would have happily stayed like that all night.

Magnify the sensation Kim had felt when simply brushing her hand at the bar way back at the party; this was something else and he had to break away, or he wouldn't be able to stop.

The Frog Theory

'*Now* can we go for that drink?'
She nodded, dumbly.

'No food fights tonight, okay?' said Flow, looking from Clea to Kim playfully, after they were settled with their round.

'Very funny, ha ha!' said Clea, blushing and sipping her drink, which had arrived with a straw in it. And more fruit than she would have expected in a gin and tonic.

'There she is, that one. Did you see her? Did she look at me?' said Flow.

Kim and Clea exchanged a glance and tried not to laugh.

'I'm not sure, Flow,' said Clea. 'She may have. I'll keep looking and let you know.'

The waitress at Bar East was completely different from Jackie – waiflike and a bit nervous. Clea noticed that she had a lovely, warm smile – and she thought she looked nice.

'Okay, I'm going to go to the loo, just watch her and see if she looks at me, all right?'

'All right,' promised Clea and Kim, both following Flow's long strides with their eyes as he walked leisurely to the gents.

'So,' said Kim. 'How have you been?' They were avoiding eye contact.

'Okay,' said Clea, carefully. Maybe just once she could spend an evening with Kim and *not* make a fool of herself, despite the shaky start and the incredible kiss, which seemed like a dream right now. 'I actually met someone in France who really *did* boil a frog!' she blurted. Damn it, why had she said that?

Kim raised an enquiring eyebrow.

'Yeah...she would go to this river with her family as a kid and they would camp and...they chucked frogs in the boiling pan sometimes, to see what happened.' She felt herself blushing, but she had started now, so she kind of had to carry on. 'She feels really bad about it...we were talking about silly things we did when we were young.' She tailed off. 'Emm hm.' She ended, chasing the straw awkwardly, before taking a self-conscious sip.

'And?'

'And what?' Damn straw, she took it out and put it on the table next to her glass, along with the strange preponderance of fruit.

'What happened? Did it jump out?'

'Well...no...it died. Every time.'

'Guess that's why it's only a *theory*,' he said, drinking more of his pint. 'Kind of disappointing, though.'

'Well?' said Flow expectantly, arriving back to the table and taking his seat.

'Go again,' said Kim. 'We forgot to look.'

'Go again? She'll think I'm incontinent.' Clea stifled a giggle and Flow reached for his pint. 'Useless,' he muttered. 'Told you she was cute, though, don't you think she's cute?' His eyes followed her around as she cleared the glasses.

Somehow his presence relaxed them both and the evening started to feel more natural. The conversation began to bubble easily and their inhibitions disappeared. Before they knew it, closing time was upon them and Flow was in a great mood, having got the waitress's number.

'Shall we check out that club everyone's always on about?' said Flow. It was only down the road under one of the railway arches and it wasn't long before they were inside, pumping music all around.

'My go for the bar,' yelled Clea over the din. They had been so generous with drinks, she was determined to get a round: lemony shooters.

'One – two – three – drink – SLAM!

And they hit the dance floor.

Whatever good energy there was in the world, an ample spattering was with them tonight in that dank London tunnel. Everything just seemed to fit into place. Relaxed, complete, no room for anything dark or sad – the music pulsed through them.

Their mood was infectious. People danced with them, they danced on the stage, they slammed more cocktails, they had a ball.

Eventually they staggered out, happy and laughing.

The Frog Theory

'We have to take her to the Glass Block, Kim,' said Flow.

'It's miles away – you're mad.'

'The kebab's not so good around here an' I don't know what it is…I kinda need a Fulham fix.'

They helped Clea up the lift shaft and onto the top of the Glass Block – they could see for miles around.

'This is our place,' said Flow, surveying the view. 'An' we have this thing, Kim and I, we trust each other…so you need to get that. You get it, I know you get it. You get it? Don't you?' he slurred.

'I don't know if I get it,' said Clea, dancing with him to some invisible song. 'Do you get it, Kim?' she called over his shoulder. 'Flow needs to know if I get it!'

They sat with the breeze blowing in their faces, the sun was about to come up.

'I'm going to kip at Mum and Dad's,' said Flow, suddenly. It had felt right that they all be together until now.

Clea gave him a bear hug goodbye. 'You still need to come to the show!' she called after him.

Alone, Kim and Clea watched the sunrise together.

'So,' said Kim eventually.

'So,' said Clea, looking at him with a smile.

Shhh. Listen to the rain

Dear Diary,

I haven't written in here for quite a while, I've been too traumatised, but my very nice counsellor said journaling was a healthy thing and I have missed you. The rain is falling so gently today, it helps me to think.

It was easy after the food fight for Hugo to find out where Clea was performing and he soon took to following her, my worst fear realised. His strange mutterings continued and on the evening before my birthday, I found him in her room sitting cross-legged on the floor, talking to her online profile like she was real. He was saying despicable things and threatening to kill her.

Even in writing it is hard to say but it is meant to help to get these things out and I want to get better. He started to pleasure himself, it was disgusting.

A colossal fury hit me. All the times he had said Clea was bad and needed disciplining for her own good had been a lie, covering his own perversions, and I had been stupid enough to believe him.

I went to our bedroom in a fug. He had hit her so many times before, what if he really did kill her? I'd hardly slept for months. I was trapped in the horror of a depressed mind and had been in close vicinity to a psychopath for years.

The Frog Theory

I picked up the baseball bat and tiptoed back to Clea's room, where he was still furiously 'at it'. I closed my eyes and hit him on the head as hard as I possibly could. I had learnt to zone out when he had been hurting Clea and I did the same thing now, so that the crack of the bat arrived at my ears only as a distant and muted thing. I didn't look, I backed away with my eyes still shut and kept going until I could feel by the walls that I was on the landing, then I turned around and ran out of the house, all the way to the Duke of Cumberland pub.

The barman was so very kind. He could see how distressed I was. 'Call the police, I think I've killed my husband,' I said.

He gave me a drink, such kindness I had not expected. I told him I had no money, but he still gave it to me. I needed it so very much, the kindness, and the drink. I told him, it's my birthday tomorrow, and sat waiting for the police.

Yes, he was dead but all I had to do was go to jail and it was a relief. I didn't have to go back to the house. They gave me a medical and diagnosed me with persistent depressive disorder, often referred to as dysthymia. They said that postnatal depression and Clea's father leaving me could have been the beginning of the more serious condition it had become.

That made sense to me, Clea's father had been so charismatic. He was rich, good-looking – what my own mother would have called a 'dream-boat'.

He broke my heart when he said he didn't love me anymore – he told me I was dull and that stung. So often my words would get lost and not come out because I loved him so much. Hugo was what my counsellor calls 'a rebound'.

The medication they gave me was completely different from that of the doctor, and the longer I take it, the clearer my thinking becomes, as my brain chemistry continues to even out.

Sometimes the past is like a high definition film, it is hard to confront the memories of the way Hugo treated Clea.

My counsellor told me that fifty seven per cent of women in here have suffered some form of domestic abuse. I told her it was Clea who had suffered but she said that I had been abused, too. I still struggle with that. It was my job to protect my daughter and for so long I failed.

I don't want to upset Clea further, I am thinking about whether to contact her or not. I see that she is doing well, she looks beautiful and happy when I find things about her online. It's uplifting and makes me swell with pride.

I got sentenced with involuntary manslaughter. I will do two years and then community service.

Incongruously, I feel happier than I ever have felt in my life — I kept my daughter safe from harm at last, I finally did my job.

No more nightmares

After their trip to Australia, a new atmosphere swept through their home. There was no longer the need to hold back or to hide, no almighty lie so monumental that it had started to become a physical thing. The nightmares had stopped and family relations had continued to get closer and warmer; though it had hit her mother hard, and Sophie was not talking to any of them right now.

Isobel's main concern was the children, not Sophie. She had been worried that they would become angry as things sank in but so far, that had not happened, and Mike had not so much as written them an email, which was confirmation that their lives were better without him.

Overall, there was a peace in her heart that she had never experienced before – so this is was what happened when you listened to your conscience?

A new term began, and a new class of students joined the college. Catching the train, she diligently scanned the carriage, looking for the man with the wedding ring. What was his story? She was ready to know. Monday, nothing. Tuesday, nothing. Wednesday. She could see him – her heart leapt and when he noticed her, she smiled.

Charlie

Charlie was so proud of Clea's progress since she had walked into his office all that time ago – his broken little bird had mended. She had been sensible enough to lean on him, as he had suggested, but never overwhelmingly so, and he was extremely fond of her.

Clea had met his daughter one evening, and they had gone to see Clea's flatmate in a show at The Old Vic, but this was the first time she had been to his home, next to the annex in South Kensington.

Sometimes people needed mirages to get them through difficult experiences, so he had let Clea keep both her distance, *and* her illusions of his happy family. The time never seemed right to tell her that his wife had died long ago. They hadn't been that happy, and the last thing he remembered was arguing with her. She said they couldn't afford for him to keep acting, that he needed to think of the children. Perhaps if she hadn't have been so angry, she wouldn't have stepped into the road like that without looking. He would give anything to go back.

Now Clea was going to come to the house at last, and wanted to introduce to him someone special. He felt he could be open and share the sad news, along with some unexpected *good*.

He had finally removed his wedding ring, slipping it carefully into the front of his wedding album, along with the past. Against all odds, he had met somebody.

They all had something to celebrate this evening.

'Darling, the young couple I told you about are here!' he called, ushering them excitedly into the sitting room. 'Would you mind grabbing the champagne?'

Clea introduced Charlie to Kim. Charlie immediately got a good feeling, the room felt light with his presence and they chatted easily, sinking into comfortable sofas.

Presently, his new love came into the room, holding the chilled bottle, ready to pour the sparkling liquid into the four glasses standing proudly on the coffee table.

She was flustered, running late after a busy day at work. She didn't mind having guests sprung on her at the last moment, but she wished she had been able to have a hot shower. Never mind, she had at least dragged a brush through her hair and had refreshed her make-up. 'Clea, Kim – I'd like to introduce you to Isobel.'

'Christ on a bike!' exclaimed the principal, nearly dropping the bottle.

The End

Epilogue

Amongst her father's belongings, Clea found some photos. There was one of him with her mother, young and in love. She felt a great surge of gratitude in her heart – at last, a moment she could be thankful for; a moment that had contributed towards bringing her here. She loved her life, she loved her work, she loved her friends, and she loved Kim.

A counsellor had been in touch, asking whether she would like to go and visit her mother in jail. She said that she would like that very much.